Justice on

STAND-ALONE NOVEL

A Western Historical Adventure Book

by

Zachary McCrae

Disclaimer & Copyright

Table of Contents

Letter from Zachary McCrae

I'm a man who loves plain things; a cup of strong coffee in the morning, a good book at noon and his wife's embrace at night. I want to write stories that take you from the hand and show you what it meant to be someone who tried to make ends meet and find their own way in 19-century United States. I've been this someone for a long time in my life, always looking for my next gig after my parents' sudden death, always finding new friends but somehow not being able to stick with 'em. It's easy to find quantity in your life but what about quality?

At the age of 50, and after my baby boy, Jeb, and my sweet daughter, Janette, went away to study East, with my sweet wife, Mrs. Maryanne Mc Crae, we moved back to my home town and my dad's ranch close to the Rockies. After a series of health issues that have brought me even closer to our Lord, I've officially started writing those stories I always loved to read. I'm tending my land and animals now with the help of Maryanne, and I'm grateful for each day I get to walk on this world we call earth. As the saying goes, "Nature gave us all something to fall back on, and sooner or later we all land flat on it," so I want to take care of it just the way it has taken care of my dad and mom, and my cousins.

My adventure stories are my legacy to my children and to all of the readers that will honor me by following my work. God bless you and your families and our land! Thank you.

Stay safe but adventurous,

Zachary McCrae

Prologue

Houma, Louisiana

July 25, 1868

Just another day. Or it should have been.

Brooks Shanton sat at the table; weathered hands squeezed tight around a tin mug of coffee. The coffee had long since grown cold as he stared at the bottle of open whiskey before him. It was a bottle he'd found on a shelf in the barn, forgotten, dusty, and laced with cobwebs, a bottle he'd set aside with the intention of never taking another drink, abandoned with pride two months ago when he'd vowed never to let another drop of liquor past his lips. A vow he'd kept.

Until today.

Tall and broad shouldered, the offspring of a generation of hard-laboring men who built the railroad across the west, he dwarfed the small front room of his two-room log cabin. He couldn't remember the last time he'd shaved, or cared to. The chestnut-brown stubble on his chin matched the uncombed hair on his head. His wrinkled dark blue trousers and mussed gray flannel shirt could do with a wash, but Brooks had ceased to care how he looked – or smelled – to others. Besides, there was no one around to care.

Brooks ached to pour the whiskey into the coffee and swill himself senseless in the worst way. He wanted it more than almost anything he'd wanted in his entire thirty years on this earth. Well, maybe. There was one other thing he wanted more – revenge.

The wall calendar from the feed store shouted the date – July 25th, 1862. He should have torn up and tossed the calendar in the fire more than five years ago. Why he'd kept the fool thing, brought it all the way from Texas to hang on a nail, he didn't know. It was always a reminder of a day he wished with all his might to forget.

Most days he could forget, losing himself in the hard work of carving a ranch from the harsh Louisiana land and bayous. Most of the time he counted off days on another calendar from *Jepson's Mercantile* in Houma. Today should have been just another day on his small ranch. Another morning to milk the cow and make sure the cattle he'd take to market in the fall were thriving. Feed the chickens, slop the hog, maybe ride out along the fence line in the south pasture. See if that last storm had taken out any scrub oak he could chop for firewood. Sure, it was just another day.

Except it wasn't. It was *the* day. The one that could still give him nightmares. Just the memory could seize him by the guts until he couldn't breathe, eat, or sleep without wanting to tear something apart. No, not some*thing*, some*one*. Three someones. It was the date that had given him an overwhelming desire to lose himself in drink. A date that cost him everything. A date he'd tried to drown in whiskey for nearly six years.

He'd expected to drink until it killed him. Each night he drank until the pain and memories went away so he could sleep – until two months ago. A freak storm came up one night after he'd drank himself to nothingness. Booming thunder tore him from the welcome oblivion of sleep. In a blur, his first thought went to Ruthie, his milk cow, ready to calf any day now. *Did I put her in the barn?* Fierce bolts of lightning scarred the sky as he fumbled from the twisted quilt, still fully dressed, stamped feet into boots and grabbed a buffalo-skin coat.

What happened in the hours after he slammed shut the log door, he could never remember completely. Ruthie was not in the barn. He'd set out to look for her and had become disoriented in the dark windy storm. The night was as black as the inside of an iron kettle. The rain, driving fierce needles of pain into his face, drenched his felt brimmed hat. Later, he knew he had gotten too close to the edge of a bayou and had fallen and hit his head. That he didn't become gator bait – or worse – could only be an act of Providence. He came to with his mouth full of brackish water, a stench of decaying weeds in his nose, and a throbbing ache in his head.

Hours later, he dragged himself inside the cabin to lie panting on the floor, thankful to be alive and breathing. In that instant, he'd vowed to stop drinking once and forever. Two months later, the date on the calendar mocked his vow.

Brooks poured a generous amount of whiskey into the coffee and took a burning swallow of the bitter liquid. *There goes two months of being sober down the drain.*

"I was the best Sheriff Beaumont ever had." He'd gotten in the habit of talking to himself. "Yes siree … the best. I used to have a nickname, *The Golden Star.* How about that?" He nodded to the whiskey, "'Course the ole' *demon rum,* as my Sunday school teacher used to say, got me where I couldn't do a good job. Too busy drinking to care about my duties."

He remembered his former deputy, Sam Rathbone, the best friend he'd ever had, except for – no, he wouldn't think of *her.* Not today. Today would be the worst day for memories, the worst date on the whole danged calendar.

He reached for the bottle of whiskey. What did it matter if he stayed sober? Last night he'd had another nightmare. Woke up screaming, like he had as a little boy. That July 25 six years ago had marked him forever. The terror, the fear, his helplessness, it never went away. Maybe it never would.

Thinking about Sam reminded Brooks it had been a good long while since he'd heard from him. He fixed his mind on remembering and realized with a start how long it had been. "Guess I should write Sam," he told himself. "Tell him I took his advice and got a ranch. Maybe wish him a happy fifty-fourth birthday." Brooks remembered Sam's birthday always came a week after ...

Stop! Don't think of her ...

Just then a frantic pounding came at the door of the cabin. Brooks stared at the door, his hand on the bottle. *Who in blazes?*

"Help! Help me! Please!"

The voice sounded young and female.

Brooks jumped up, knocking over the wooden chair, and strode to the door. He pulled it open just as the woman on the other side lifted her hand to pound again. The sudden motion caused her to stumble forward, almost dropping the baby perched on one hip. Brooks got one startled glance at the greenest eyes he'd ever seen, set in a tear-streaked, flushed face covered with dirt and bloody scratches.

The woman fell through the doorway. "H-h-elp me, please!"

Brooks only just had time to snatch the baby up in one arm before the woman lunged forward, stumbled again, and collapsed in a puddle of sprigged green calico on the dusty wooden floor.

Just another day? Maybe not.

Chapter One

Earlier That Day

July 25, 1868

Near Houma, Louisiana

"*'Steal a baby from an orphanage,'* they said! *'You'll do it if you know what's good for you.'*"

Nineteen-year-old Hattie Munn stumbled down the dusty road, hampered by a long green calico dress and petticoats. She couldn't remember the last time she'd worn a skirt; she usually wore pants like all the others. It felt a mite strange to be walking along like any other woman, in a dress and sunbonnet. The stolen baby in her arms gurgled and patted Hattie's sunburned cheek, tugging on Hattie's sunbonnet strings.

A baby! What am I doing with a baby?

"You know, Olive, I should have said I'm not doin' it."

A small voice babbled back at her. "Ma, ma?"

The night before, Hattie had managed to fool the old lady running the orphanage. She'd cried and screamed bloody murder, sobbing that a gang had attacked her. It had fooled the matron so well, she gave Hattie a room for the night, promising to send for a sheriff in the morning. Left alone, Hattie had all the time in the world to sneak into the room where the babies slept and take her pick, and to grab up some little baby dresses and some diaper flannels. It was easy as pie to climb out a window with her small bundle, mount a waiting horse and get clean away, then to find the others and show them she'd done as they ordered. *I stole a baby, just like you told me.*

10

The little girl, perched on Hattie's hip, grinned at her with sweet blue eyes and a gap-toothed smile. Two little pearly teeth showed in the top of her mouth. Wisps of blond ringlets curled around dainty little ears.

Hattie sighed. Her hair was blond, too, but cut short so no one could take her for a girl.

Hattie had decided to name the baby Olive. Wasn't no particular reason; it was just a name she fancied. Hattie had such a dull, brown-sounding name, almost like a cow's name. *Olive* sounded fine and pretty. Once, Hattie had seen a fancy lady in Beaumont, dressed in a green silk dress. A gentleman had helped her out of a buggy and called her "Miss Olive." Oh, how rich and fine it sounded!

"I reckon if you got to be stole from an orphanage, the least I can do is give you a pretty name," Hattie told the baby. "Yes, sirree, Olive, I should have told *him* I'm not takin' no baby from an orphanage."

Hattie sighed, knowing she'd never be brave enough to refuse any of them. Especially *him.*

"You better do what I say, or else!"

Hattie didn't need a reminder of what *or else* would mean. In the years since she'd been with the gang, she'd known a lot of *or else.* A sharp smack across the face, a switch to the backs of her legs ... or worse. Sometimes she didn't get to eat or have a cool drink of water for days. Hattie could remember thirst so powerful her tongue curled in on itself. As long as they tolerated her, it was best not to rile them. Where else could she go? Hattie had long since hardened her heart to wishing for any other life. *What good would it do? Although maybe – this time – if I do good, I'll be free.*

Dang this sunbonnet! The sun burned overhead, so she struggled to keep it in place, but it didn't fit her head in the

11

same easy way the well-worn sombrero had. This sunbonnet twisted like a demon thing. If it didn't pitch forward over her eyes, it near about strangled her when it flopped down her back, the strings taut against her throat. It was probably almost like being hung – something Hattie hoped never to find out.

"Wonder if stealin' a baby counts as a hanging offense," she asked Olive. "You reckon it's the worst thing that could happen if we get caught?"

'Cept maybe even the worst that could happen would be better than where she found herself now. *Louisiana. What kind of a place is this?*

"Gimme Texas any day," she told the baby babbling in her aching arms. "Soon as we do what we gotta do, we can go back to Texas, and I won't never leave again. Ever."

Hattie couldn't remember any home other than Beaumont, Texas. 'Course, maybe when she had a Ma, she'd lived somewhere else. That was too far back to remember, though. It wasn't the kind of question she could ask *them*. They said *do,* and she did. "I'm never leaving Texas again," she repeated. "No sirree."

Hattie knew well enough she might not be able to keep that promise – not to herself, or the baby – if he had his way. If he told her to go to Louisiana or anywhere else, she went.

Just like he'd told her to steal this baby.

Hattie stopped, shifting Olive from one hip to another. Who knew a baby could be so heavy, or a few miles so long?

Strange old place. Hattie shivered, despite the heat blistering the top of her head through the sunbonnet. The trees along this path were live oak – she knew that much – but they had gray-green strands of cobweb stuff hanging from the branches. Every slight breeze made the strands wiggle like mossy snakes.

Hattie skirted the path through the trees, staying away from the straggly strands as much as possible. What if they really *were* snakes, or worse? She exhaled a thankful breath when the trail opened, and she could see the beginning of a wagon path. Hattie stepped gratefully onto the grass between the ruts where the wheels had worn grooves.

The baby whimpered and grabbed Hattie's arm. Probably hungry or thirsty. Again. Or wet. Hattie felt a damp spot on her side where the baby's bottom perched. Babies sure were a lot of trouble. Be nice if you could just put them out in a pasture like a horse and have them fend for themselves.

Sighing, Hattie dropped a threadbare satchel and reached into the pocket of the green rose-patterned dress to pull out a piece of jerky. She put it between her teeth and bit off a length. The rest she put into the baby's fisted hand. The baby's bright, blue eyes stared at the strange food, but it didn't take more than a second for the jerky strip to find her mouth. As near as Hattie could tell, the baby liked the dried beef, just like she had a while ago. Jerky shouldn't hurt her none. *But what do I know about babies?*

"Guess you was hungry, huh? Only thing I know about babies is how to steal one," she said through a mouthful of jerky. The salty taste burned, and she realized how dry her mouth felt. "Wish we had more water. An' I guess a baby ought to have milk soon."

Hattie picked up the satchel, shifted Olive to her other hip and started to walk again. *Golly, how my feet ache!* The canteen she'd been given hours before, when they dropped her off a few miles away from the Sheriff's house, had run dry. She and the baby had taken tiny sips, but it was such a hot day, and they'd gotten so thirsty walking along that it hadn't lasted long. Hattie hadn't seen a nearby stream or watering hole to refill the canteen. They'd passed a big place about two miles back – what Hattie thought people called a plantation – but she hadn't dared ask anyone for milk. "Guess when we get to that sheriff's ranch, he'll give us water. If we ever get there."

Hattie squinted up at the sky. It was going on supper time, the sun making its downward slant to the land. It had taken longer to walk from the road than she'd figured.

They'd walked another few minutes when Hattie stumbled up a small rise. Off to her right, a sturdy split-rail fence ran down into a valley. A small but well-built log cabin nestled near a tiny barn, henhouse, and a few other outbuildings. Smoke curled in a lazy drift from the chimney. It was exactly where they'd told her it would be.

"We're here," she said to Olive.

Setting the baby on the ground, Hattie took a few seconds to bend over, rub her hands in the dirt, and smear it over her face. She pulled at the ripped sleeve to widen the tear, hearing the orders barked at her earlier today.

"You got to look like you've been attacked!"

That had been right before someone slashed her right cheek with jagged fingernails. It hurt like the devil, and Hattie had felt tears burn her eyes. But she knew better than to cry. To show weakness.

They didn't like weakness. *I wished I never had to see any of them again.*

Hattie swallowed a knot of fear and gritted her teeth. Picking Olive up, she perched the baby on her hip. For just a second, she stopped, heart pounding. Her legs trembled beneath the ripped calico skirt. Once she walked up and knocked on the door, everything would fly into motion like a dust devil whirling before the wind. It would all come about just like he said. Everything would happen like it should until the sheriff got what was coming to him.

Hattie didn't particularly care what happened to the man named Brooks Shanton. She didn't know him. The man in the cabin was just someone she had to convince so *he* got his way. No one dared to flout his plans and she didn't aim to be the first. Hattie had seen what happened to others who'd tried to defy him. If she couldn't do this right, it might almost be better to just get hung and have it over.

Still, it didn't keep her from being scared spitless or keep her heart from going *pittypat, pittypat* like a galloping mare.

"Reckon this is it, Olive." Sucking in a deep breath she took off running toward the cabin. A lady running for her life would, of course, run. Hattie's boots clattered up the two wooden steps onto the porch. Dropping the worn satchel, she raised her fist and pounded at the cabin door with all her might.

"Help me! Help me!"

Wasn't no way to stop that dust devil plan from rollin' on now. Not until Brooks Shanton ended up a dead man.

Chapter Two

Dazed by the unexpected entrance, Brooks, a damp baby in his left arm, stared at the heap of woman on his cabin floor. A green calico skirt spread out like a puddle around her as a shabby canteen plunked from her shoulder. Worry creased his forehead. *Was she hurt? Dead?*

He shook his head, trying to clear the haze from his mind. Suddenly he was glad that he had only taken a few drinks of whiskey, not enough to dull his senses entirely. *Maybe that's what it took to sober up? A strange woman landing at my feet.*

"Ma'am?" he asked, bending over. *Is she breathing? Did she swoon?* As the sheriff of Beaumont, he'd had to deal once or twice with a swooning woman. It always left him stammering, shifting from boot to boot. Wasn't like you could just pick up a woman and toss her somewhere like you could a man. Give him a regular bank robbery any day. A robbery he could deal with. A fainting woman made him feel like he'd jumped in a pond over his head and forgotten how to swim. "Ma'am, are you hurt?"

As he watched, she sat up, brushing a few loose strands of short yellow hair from her face. Brooks wondered if she'd had a fever and had to cut it off. He saw those green eyes again. Brooks felt like maybe he might drown after all; he shook his head to get hold of himself. *This woman's in trouble. No time to wonder how pretty she'd be with that yellow hair clean and shining and those dirt smudges wiped off her face.*

Brooks felt a protective instinct take over and he reached out a hand to help her up. "Can you stand? Let me help you to a chair."

"A chair?" She whispered, then whimpered. "H-h-help me. I was never so s-s-scared!" The last word came out in a wail as she buried her face in her hands. "They chased me! I ran and ran and ran! Help me! Don't let them find me!"

"Surely, ma'am." He'd just reached out a hand when the baby took that second to wail. The instinct he'd had from all those years ago kicked in and he joggled the baby on his hip. *Cute little feller.* Even with brown drool across his face and muddy tear streaks, those eyes were bright blue and full of mischief. *Just like ...* Brooks snapped his mind shut like a bear trap, remembering the date.

"Here." He tried to thrust the baby toward her. "Guess the little feller wants his mama. Just let me help you to a chair."

The woman shook her head, cradled the canteen to her body and managed to stand fine on her own, like she hadn't just fallen to his floor. Or pounded on his door, screaming for help. Like they were having a *howdy-how-you-been* conversation beside the general store in Houma. Not like she'd just told him she was scared, being chased.

Something's not right here.

"Her. Olive, that's her name. Just set her down. Probably wants somethin'. Babies is always wanting something."

Puzzled, Brooks sat Olive on the floor. The baby whined, sniffing away a few last tears. Spying a newspaper he'd tossed on the floor, the baby crawled toward it. Little fingers grabbed and began to rip the pages in a delightful game. *Well, no matter.* He'd read it ten times already. Might keep Olive busy so he could find out what was wrong with her mama.

The woman walked on steady legs to a wooden chair and plunked down. Despite those sparkling eyes and heart shaped face, her words came out coarse, tough. Certainly not fearful. "You got any water? That sun out there was mighty hot. My canteen went dry miles ago."

As if she'd just remembered the canteen, the woman pulled the strap from her arm and placed it on the wooden table. Her eyes glanced at the bottle of whiskey sitting there, to him and back to the bottle. Not a word of reproach passed her lips. Not even a frown crossed her face. Brooks didn't know many women who didn't feel honor bound to remark on the "demon rum." Whether it was their business or not.

A sense of unease stirred in Brooks. He'd been a sheriff long enough to feel what he called 'barbed wires of doubt' about people. His old deputy, Sam Rathbone, would say he had a natural born instinct about people. "Yup," Sam used to say, "you can smell a lie like most people smell cow manure."

"I'm mighty thirsty," she repeated.

"Water? Sure ..." Brooks went to the pail of well water he'd drawn earlier that morning. He filled a dipper and handed it to the woman. The woman – who, on a closer look, was barely more than a girl – took the dipper and drank like she'd been parched for hours. While she drank, Brooks took the whiskey, plugged in the cork and placed it on the rough wooden shelves he'd made for his dishes and canned goods.

"More?"

Brooks filled the dipper twice before the girl had her fill and sat back satisfied. Oddly, she swiped an arm across her mouth just like a man. "Do you want to give Olive a drink?"

"You can. Probably she's thirsty too. You got any milk? She might like some milk? Ain't that what babies drink most – milk?"

Strange. While he'd know a few mamas who weren't all that motherly, most cared for their young in some way. Most mamas would have given the baby a drink before they helped themselves. And surely even the most uneducated mother knew babies needed milk.

"I'll milk in a bit. She's welcome to all she can drink."

He filled the dipper halfway and walked over to the baby. As he got closer, he realized she'd soiled her diaper. He squatted down and held the dipper. Olive gulped water like she couldn't get enough. It spilled down her face and onto the well-worn and mended white dress she wore. When she'd had her fill, she grinned a gap-toothed smile. *Pretty little thing.* It put Brooks in mind of other baby faces, other baby smiles. Just like a knife through his heart.

"Little Olive smells a bit ripe," he said with a smile as the baby crawled off to rip more paper. "Maybe you want to clean her up?" *And yourself,* he wanted to add.

Fact is, he thought, *I guess I smell a mite ripe myself. Wasn't expecting a lady to show up at my door today. Maybe I could even do with a shave. Although from the looks of her, we sure make a fine pair. Like neither one of us has seen the likes of a brush or washcloth any time recently.*

He studied the woman closely. Dirt streaked her face and hands. A few bloody scratches marred her right cheek. The worn green calico had rips at the shoulders and across the skirt. Brooks had to avert his eyes from the pale skin of the woman's bare shoulder through the tear. A wrinkled sunbonnet flopped down her back. While she looked mussed, grubby even, she didn't look as if she'd run for her life. "I can heat up some water. Won't take but a few minutes to build up a fire."

The woman waved a limp hand as she yanked off the sunbonnet. "In a while. I never was so tired in all my life. I bet I walked near about ten miles. After I got away from those men …" Her voice got low, and she glanced at the cabin door – still hanging open after her unexpected arrival. "You reckon they followed me here? I never was so scared. Please, mister, can we stay here? Just until I'm sure they're gone." Again, she managed tears and mopped her eyes with the sunbonnet. "An' we're so hungry, me and the babe. We ain't had anything but jerky. You got anything we can eat? I ain't got no money to pay but I'm right handy with chores."

"Poor little Olive," she smiled in a tender way toward the baby but didn't seem to care she was chewing pieces of newsprint and spitting them out. "Reckon her stomach's about to turn inside out bein' so hungry."

Brooks wondered for the first time if the woman was *loco*. First, she was scared; then she wasn't. As a sheriff he had seen some mighty strange reactions when people were attacked, though. Like the time he'd come upon a wagon train attacked by marauders. People dead all around, even the oxen slaughtered, but one woman sat there in a rocking chair, singing, and knitting away at a shawl with bloody yarn. "Some people can't take in the enormity of what they lost," old Doc Matthews said when they'd got the woman into town. "Their minds just shut out the bad and they act on something good and regular." Maybe this woman couldn't take it all in either. If she *had* been attacked, he needed to know.

How and why.

Brooks pulled another wooden chair around and sat down across from the woman. "I can fix supper and get some milk for the baby, but first, Ma'am, if you don't mind, I think we need to talk. My name's Brooks Shanton. I used to be a sheriff in Beaumont, Texas. You and the baby are safe here. I won't let anyone trouble you, but I need to know more about what happened. Who were these men who chased you?"

"Sure enough?" She ignored his questions. "Ain't that a wonder. That's where I was goin'. Beaumont, Texas."

The baby gagged on the newspaper. Mama jumped up, snatched up the baby and held her tight. "Now why'd you eat that for, Olive? You spit that out." She seemed to have trouble figuring out how to get the baby to open her mouth to pull out the damp wad of paper, then soothe the tearful Olive. Then an ungainly amount of time to shift the baby around on a hip, like it was a new skill she hadn't mastered yet. "We're gonna eat soon."

Startled, Brooks stared at the woman, watched her sit back down, struggling to get the baby to sit quietly on her lap. He pushed a spoon across to the baby who grabbed it up with chubby fingers. "You were on your way to Beaumont?" The only question he could think to ask was, "Why?"

"I was goin' to my aunt's house. She wrote me and Olive could come live with her."

"What's your aunt's name? I might know her. I grew up in Beaumont, lived there all my life."

"No, you wouldn't know her. She ain't been there long, only about two years."

How do you know I wasn't there two years ago?

"What's her name anyway? And yours?" He thought to ask. "I know your baby's name, but not yours."

This time she laughed, right out loud. *Curious.* "I guess we ain't been proper introduced. Hattie Munn. Same as my aunt's. Her name's Hattie too. Guess Ma figured it best to name me after somebody in the family."

Hattie Munn. The name sounded familiar somehow, but if he'd ever heard it, his mind refused to remind him where. "No, I guess I don't know her. Although there's something familiar about it." The name taunted his memory for half a second, then vanished. "You say you were going to meet her?"

21

Hattie nodded. "Me and Olive was coming out on the stagecoach." Again, her eyes glittered with tears and her hands trembled. For a minute Brooks thought she might reach across the table and grab his hands, but she didn't. "That's when those men – oh, it was terrible! I thought they'd have their way with me! I was never so scared."

The stagecoach? Odd this woman mentioned the stage. Brooks knew the nearest route was a good fifteen miles away. There was no way she could have walked or run that far carrying a baby. It had to be over 90 degrees today. By the looks of Hattie's worn clothes and the baby's, she didn't appear to have the money for a fare. Unless the aunt had sent it to her. *If* there was an aunt.

"Were you traveling alone? Unchaperoned? Just you and the baby? What about your husband, Hattie? Why wasn't he with you?"

"I ain … he's dead." Hattie stated, those green eyes almost daring him to contradict her, mouth set in a firm line.

So, she didn't have a husband. Maybe that's why she was coming to live with an aunt. It made sense in a sorry kind of way. Still, Brooks felt those *barbed wires of doubt*. Something about Hattie's story didn't make sense.

Brooks had never heard of anyone sending a young woman with a baby over the treacherous Louisiana roads, around the bayous, on a stage. Not alone and unchaperoned. It just wasn't done. No stage driver he knew would have allowed it.

"Were the men who attacked you on the stage?"

A fearful nod.

There was another part of the story that didn't add up. Brooks couldn't see old Mr. Dupont, who drove the Houma mail stage, allowing four men to attack a defenseless woman with a baby. He was a skilled shot and had stopped bandits more than once with his Winchester – a relic of the war between the states.

"Can you tell me what happened?"

This time there were no tears. Just a shaky voice as Hattie told the story. "Well, me 'n Olive was on the stagecoach, going to my aunt's. We stopped somewhere so they could water the horses. That's when ..." This time she did grasp one hand in the other and shake as if remembering the horror of it all. "These men, maybe four or five, started to chase me. I said they could take all my money if they was a mind to, just don't hurt me or Olive. But they just laughed and tore my dress. The one, he scratched my face." Hattie lifted trembling fingers to the scratches on her cheek. "That's when I knew I had to run and get away. So, I did. They chased me for a while, but I hid out in a fallen log. Then I found a road an' kept walking until I saw your smoke. An' I thought maybe someone here could help me."

Odd. If she'd walked – or run – all the way from the stagecoach route, she'd have had to pass by the Overview Plantation and its fields of sugar cane, or the other nearest neighbor, the Landry's – a Cajun family who fished for a living and often brought Brooks supplies from town. If she needed help, why pass up those places?

"I can help you," Brooks said out loud, but inside he thought, *who are you, Hattie Munn, and why are you here?*

Chapter Three

In the western sky, a wash of pink, orange, and deep red set fire to the close of day. A flock of scrawny hens clucked and bunched across the dusty yard. In one of the pastures, the Brahma cattle lowed, settling down to sleep. A whinny and the chatter of night insects signaled chore time.

"Make yourself at home," Brooks told Hattie as he grabbed up the dark felt-brimmed hat he'd worn as Sheriff. Clapping it on his head, he said, "There's ham and eggs, if you want to build up the fire and start supper. I'll get milk for Olive and be in after chores." His eyes narrowed speculatively, almost as if he aimed to say more, then pressed his lips tight and headed outside.

He closed the cabin door, took a step, and tripped over a worn rose-patterned satchel. *Is this yours ...* The words and his motion to go back inside halted. It had to belong to Hattie. *Might be a good idea to see what she carries inside – while running for her life.*

Brooks strode off the porch accompanied by half a dozen clucking white hens and Absalom, the lone rooster, preening his black and white feathers. The chickens scattered around his long legs as he headed toward the barn.

The small, sturdy log barn held stalls for the milk cow, her calf, and his stallion, Midnight, plus a few grain bins to hold the animal's feed. He'd bought the whole ranch, ready-made, from a man who'd called it quits and headed to Ohio. Brooks thanked Providence for that favor, and Sam, who'd put the idea into his head to leave Texas. His old deputy had talked him into taking advantage of the Homestead Act in '62.

"Go somewheres new, Brooks," he'd suggested. "Get away from all the heartache and such. Get yourself a ranch, and forget being Sheriff. I heard tell the government's givin' away free land if you stake a claim an' stay on it five years. You was always talking about having a few cattle, a little ranch somewhere."

Although Brooks had taken the suggestion, being able to build a working ranch too drunk to hold a hammer was a different matter. Finding a ready-made cabin, barn, and outbuildings, plus miles of fenced-in pasture was a gift he couldn't refuse. The Ohio gent had also sold him most of the stock, including a fine herd of Brahma cattle.

"How ya doing, Ruth?" he asked the brown, milking Shorthorn. Ruth mooed a reply, nudging him with her solid head. Brooks sat the worn satchel on a bale of hay and set about his evening chores. Time enough to search through it later.

It didn't take long to milk Ruth; she still had a calf to feed, a calf she'd given birth to after that stormy night two months ago. Brooks hadn't thought of a name for the little heifer yet. The calf, a tawny brown like her mama, shied away from him, hiding behind Ruth. "Guess this'll have to do," he said as he poured milk into a cracked saucer for the barn cat.

"Looks like enough for Olive tonight. Hattie, too, if she's of a mind to drink it."

Hattie. He sure couldn't get the sight of those green eyes out of his mind, nor her strange answers to his questions. Brooks didn't know what to believe of her story. *A pretty young thing, alone in this hostile country, with a baby.* Something was not quite right about that, but he couldn't put a finger on what it meant. His brown eyes stared at the gray siding of the barn in uneasy puzzlement.

I've sure never heard of a person running for their life taking time to snatch up a satchel. Running away from danger, toting a baby too, but she thought to grab her bag and a canteen. Does that make a lick of sense? Grabbing up Olive sure, to keep the baby safe. But a carpetbag? A canteen? Just who were those men chasing her – if there were men?

A furrow of worry creased his forehead as went into the barn and grabbed the bag. Mindful to hide his actions, in case Hattie happened to look out a window, he untied the rope handles that held the carpetbag shut. *Sure is a poor excuse for a travelin' bag.* The rose-patterned sides were worn threadbare in spots. At one time it must have had leather handles, but those were long gone. Just holding the sorry-looking thing touched his heart in a way he hadn't felt in a long time.

Poor little thing. What kind of a man would leave her with a child and abandon her? Such a pretty – Now, you stop right there, Brooks Shanton! Don't go letting yourself feel sorry for this woman. Not until you know more about her.

Accompanied by quiet munching from Ruth, he riffled through the bag's contents. Not much – a few little baby dresses, a couple of diaper flannels, a pair of worn men's pants and a soft, loose shirt. A sombrero, folded in two and tied closed with a length of string. No women's clothes at all. None of those soft, muslin underclothes women wore. No corset. No chemise. No ... Brooks blushed, remembering the feel of soft undergarments under his calloused hands. Not Hattie's, but ... the only woman who had claimed his heart.

He gritted his teeth, reaching to feel the bottom of the bag. Nothing else. Most women, he recalled, traveled with a handkerchief, a brush, all those female fripperies. Hattie had nothing. Again, his heart clenched with pity.

Brooks finished his evening chores in an absent-minded way. Those barbed wires of doubt pricked in his mind in the worst way. *Where did you come from, Hattie? Why are you here? Were you sent to draw me out somehow?*

He'd just stopped at the spring house to get a mound of butter when a shrill scream ripped through the dusk.

A sickening wave of terror rushed through Brooks' belly.

NO! Not again!

***

Once Brooks left to do the evening chores, Hattie got busy. She took kindling and the scraps of paper Olive had torn to shreds and started a fire in the large black Franklin stove. Sure would be a pleasure to cook on a wood stove and not over a campfire for a change. Once the wood began to crackle, she added a smaller log and then another. After that she poured water from the drinking pail into the blue enamel coffeepot on the stove. There were small boxes and linen bags on the wooden shelves. Hattie searched until she discovered the coffee in a small wooden box and added it to the pot.

Ham and eggs! Hattie's mouth watered at the thought. It'd been a long time since she'd eaten that jerky. A hank of smoked ham hung from a nail near the door. The eggs sat in an enamel bowl on a dry sink. A couple of cast iron skillets hung from nails. *This Brooks must be rich to have all this for his own self.* Hattie couldn't imagine having a whole ham and bowl of eggs – ten of them – just for one person.

Used to cooking and making do, Hattie searched the dusty, cobweb-festooned room until she found a tin of lard. It didn't take long to slice chunks of ham and set them to fry in a skillet of lard. A search in the wooden barrels, lined up under the wooden shelves, produced flour, sugar, cornmeal and salt. A few wooden bowls sat on another shelf with a sparse set of tin dishes. She took a bowl down, dusted it out with a linen cloth and set about mixing up biscuits. Hattie had learned to cook at seven, and been doing it all those years since. It was one of the reasons the gang kept her around – to cook, wash up, fetch, and carry. Without those skills, she wasn't sure she'd have a place. It didn't bear thinking about.

Who else would take you in, Hattie Munn? Your own Ma didn't want you.

The scent of frying ham filled the room. From outside the glass windows – real glass, Hattie noticed, not just a linen cloth or oilcloth – chickens clucked, and a horse whinnied.

"You hungry, baby?"

Olive began to fret and stood on unsteady bare feet; the little white dress mussed with half the floor's dirt. "Da, da, muk, muk," she babbled and lurched toward Hattie. Aware of the heat from the stove, Hattie looked around for somewhere to put the baby. There was another room behind a closed door, but she didn't want to put the baby out of sight. Plus, she smelled like rotten …

Darn, that soiled diaper. Hattie knew babies wore such things as diapers, but until yesterday, she had no idea how to put them on. It had only been chance she grabbed up a couple of little dresses and some linen squares when she swiped Olive from the orphanage. *'Steal a baby,' they said. Didn't say 'make sure she's got clothes.'*

Hattie pressed her lips tight, trying not to think back to that night when *he* told her she had to steal a baby. No questions. No balking. Just steal a baby so she'd look like a "respectable" woman when she met Brooks. Nobody figured out a baby weren't like an animal, couldn't just take her and keep her bunched up in a satchel to pull out. A baby had to have care – care Hattie didn't know how to give.

The baby had worn a linen square, tied in knots at her hips. Figuring it out as she went along, Hattie had changed one of the squares last night and again this morning. Those squares didn't stay clean an' dry long. Although she tossed the first one into some bushes last night, it didn't take long to realize they needed to be washed and dried, or the babe would be naked as a jaybird before long. *Don't reckon diapers grown on trees. Sure is a lot about babies I reckon I need to learn.*

For the first time, Hattie wondered about Olive. What would happen to her once they got to Beaumont? Had Rafael figured out how to get her back to the orphanage? A pang pierced Hattie's heart at the idea. As much trouble as Olive turned out to be, the babe had opened up an unknown place in her heart. Made her feel kind of happy, like the way she felt when the gang went off on a raid and left her alone at camp.

"Guess we better get you cleaned up right quick," she told Olive. A tin pan sat on the top of the stove; Hattie poured the last of the water into it. "We'll heat up water and get you clean again. Maybe get myself cleaned up, too ..."

I must look terrible. Mud all over my face. Hattie looked at her wavery reflection in the tin pan of water. Hattie chuckled to herself, thinking of the bearded man who'd opened the door to her. "Don't he smell a mite ripe too, Olive? An' that rat's nest he's got for hair." *But, sure, it was a deep chestnut brown, and those eyes of his – such a piercing look he gave me. What must Brooks think of me?*

"Sure, and why do you care, Hattie Munn?" she asked herself. *He's the enemy. You just got to get him back to Beaumont an' your job's done.* Hattie figured she understood that well enough in her head. Except, he sure did seem kind. Sad-eyed about something, she could tell, but still calm – gentle, almost, the way he took to Olive – an' trying to deaden the pain with drink. She'd seen enough of *that*.

Hattie sighed. If Rafael had his way, Brooks Shanton wouldn't live long. That's how it had to be if she wanted to go on livin'. *You best just keep that in mind, girl.*

"Come'ere, Olive. Let's get you cleaned up."

Olive didn't like that idea at all. She gave Hattie a merry chase around the wooden table, hiding under it, until the diaper fell and tripped her. The baby flopped down on her stomach and screamed bloody murder.

"Well, now ... why'd you go and do that ..."

The door to the cabin burst open and slammed against the wall.

Chapter Four

Brooks bolted inside; milk sloshed from the pail to the floor.

"What's wrong? What happened?"

Startled by the door thundering into the wall, Hattie gave a startled gasp and grabbed Olive to her chest in a protective embrace. "Land sakes! You scared me!"

Olive screamed louder, hiding her face against Hattie's shoulder. Little fists grabbed the calico dress and a hunk of Hattie's hair, holding on tight. Fear curled her up tight against Hattie for protection, like a little animal.

"Why'd she scream?" Brooks demanded, peered around the room, eyes wild. Ready to fight, to save. Blood pounded in his ears. Only trouble was, his hands were filled with an awkward load of carpetbag handles, milk pail and a small dish of covered butter. His fingers itched to fling it all to the floor and grab his gun from the holster on a peg.

"I reckon she don't want me to clean her up," Hattie answered, pulling Olive's clenched fist away from her hair. "She tripped an' hurt her knee. Shush, now, it's all right. Ain't nobody gonna hurt you."

For the first time since he'd heard the scream, Brooks felt his galloping heart slow down and his breathing ease back to normal. "When I heard her scream, I thought she was in danger or you, just like my wi–" The word died on his lips. "I'm sorry. I heard the scream and thought ..."

I never heard them scream. If they did ...

Hattie glanced at him with a peculiar expression on her face.

31

No danger here, Brooks. Calm down.

He sat the milk pail and butter dish on the table but kept one hand on the rope handles of the carpetbag. "I've brought some milk and butter. And I found this on the porch. This yours, ma'am?"

"Sure enough." Hattie reached around a snuffling Olive to grasp the rope handles. "Right in time, too. Got Olive an' my clothes inside. I was just tryin' to find somewhere to lay her down, clean her up."

Brooks sighed, pulled off his hat and hung it on a peg beside the door.

"Here," Brooks went to the closed door and opened it onto a small bedroom. "You and the baby can sleep in here. I'll make a pallet in front of the fire tonight."

"Thank you, kindly," she said. "Don't want to put you out none."

"Well, can't expect a lady to sleep on the floor," he said, aware that his face grew warm. *If she wiped that mud off her face, she'd be a right pretty sight to look at.* "And it's getting on toward dark, not sure where else you could go tonight. Tomorrow, maybe we can figure out something else."

The room held an iron bed, all mussed with a tangle of dirty sheets and a rumpled pink patchwork crumpled to the floor. A cedar chest sat at the foot of the bed, and an oak chest of drawers stood off to the side. In one corner, a fine walnut rocking chair sat by the window. The mirror on the dresser caught sight of them standing in the doorway: Brooks, tall and straight, and Hattie, with her mussed hair and torn dress. A small gasp burst from her lips. Whether it was from seeing herself or the sorry state of the bedroom, he wasn't sure. A glance at his reflection told him he'd sure better shave soon or he'd look like a bearded mountain man.

"Here, you can lay her on the bed to clean her up." He shuffled into the room, snatching up a pair of linen pants, a sweat-stained shirt, and a couple of empty whiskey bottles; embarrassed by the mess, he wondered where he'd last seen his broom. "Don't clean in here too often," he apologized. "Just me around, don't see much use." As if he could make up somehow for the dirty room, he yanked off the wrinkled, soiled sheets from the bed. "I got clean sheets. A washerwoman down Overview Plantation does them up for me. I'll get them for you when you're ready to make up the bed."

He motioned Hattie to come inside. The baby let Hattie's hair loose and gave little grunts of irritation. Hattie took an awkward step past him and sat a squirming Olive on the straw tick mattress.

"Let me get some warm water and cloths."

While Hattie struggled with the knots on the linen diaper, he came back with a bowl of warm water, a sliver of lye soap and a couple of clean cloths. "You can take your time washing up," he said. "I'll turn the ham and cook some eggs. Saw you mixed up some biscuits. I'll put them in the oven."

"You don't need to do that," Hattie spoke quickly, almost as if she feared his reply. "It won't take me more'n a minute to clean up the baby. You shouldn't have to cook."

"No trouble. I batch for myself all the time. You take your time." He gave her a timid smile, then tripped over his feet backing out the door. *Stop looking at those green eyes.* "Be nice to have biscuits for a change. Usually, I don't bother with baking."

He closed the door.

***

Hattie took a deep breath and dropped the carpetbag on the bed.

"Olive, Olive, Olive," she said for want of anything else to say. A cold fist closed over her heart. "He seems right kind, don't he?"

It wasn't easy to wrestle the baby to lie still on the bed. Hattie felt like she was trying to rope a calf or brand stolen cattle. The baby squalled and carried on the whole time Hattie washed her bottom clean and tied on a new diaper.

"There, run around if you've a mind," Hattie told the struggling baby as she stood her down. Olive darted off, pulled at the round wooden handles of the dresser, and babbled in baby talk.

Taking another clean rag, Hattie dipped it in the warm water and washed her face as she stared into the mirror. It had been a long, long time since Hattie had seen herself in a looking glass. Maybe as long as four years ago, when the gang had stayed in a hotel near Dallas. That night, Hattie had used the looking glass and a borrowed pair of scissors to cut her blonde hair short, as short as a boy. She still didn't like to remember the reasons why ...

Safer to look like a boy ...

Once she'd washed the mud from her face, Hattie pushed her short hair back behind her ears. There was a brush – a woman's brush, she noticed – on top of the dresser. Taking her time and enjoying the feel of the brush against her scalp, Hattie brushed her hair. If it grew out some, she might look right pretty. If she wanted to look pretty.

"You reckon he thinks I look pretty?" She whispered to herself. Embarrassed, she stared at the green calico dress, the tear in the right shoulder with her shoulder peeking through. She tried to push the torn edge into the seam, but it would need mending. *Sure was a pretty dress too. Probably stole from some woman's clothesline. All part of the plan.*

Hattie sneered at her face in the mirror. *Plan, ha! His plan, not mine.*

The warm, comforting scent of fried ham wafted under the door. Hattie's stomach rumbled. "Come on, Olive, let's go eat."

"Well, that smells mighty good." She smiled, carrying Olive into the front room.

Brooks stood at the stove, turning the eggs with a fork. He gave her a timid smile. "I've brought in a little butter too."

He poured milk in a tin cup and handed it to her, "Why don't you give Olive a few drinks to get her started."

The baby's tiny fists closed around the cup as she drank, not wanting to give it up even when it was empty. "Muk, muk."

So that's what she was trying to say. Olive wiggled in Hattie's arms, so she put her down. Off she went, toddling like a drunken cowboy around the room.

Hattie grinned to herself as she watched Brooks fork over a slice of ham to brown. Looked like he'd changed his shirt to a wrinkled tan one and washed a bit. When he walked near her, she could smell the unmistakable scent of lye soap.

Brooks had placed two blue enamel plates and forks on the table. Hattie hurried to spread them out and take the biscuits out of the tiny oven. She bumped into Brooks, red faced, and almost dropped the pan of biscuits; only his quick grab saved them from falling. Hattie gasped and cringed, pulling back, and waited for a rough slap or shouted curses at her clumsy ways.

"Here, you sit down and rest, let me dish up something. Bet you're tired from walking so far."

He sat the pan of biscuits on top of the stove.

Crouched by the side of the table, hands clenched in the folds of her skirt, Hattie couldn't fathom this. *What kind of man was this? Am I having a dream?* Hattie dropped down in one of the wooden chairs, waiting for punishment. None came. Brooks scooped up a slice of crisp fried ham, a couple of over-easy eggs, and a biscuit to put on her plate. He sat the plate on the table. Hattie waited, expecting it to be snatched away or thrown to the floor, but no … He put his own food on a plate and sat down across from her.

Reaching for a biscuit, he knifed up a scoop of the butter he'd brought in. "Guess it seems peculiar, but I love butter." He passed the plate to her along with a knife. "Not bad for a vice, huh? I eat it on everything when I've got it."

"You churn?" The question came out before Hattie could think of anything better to ask. Somehow the idea of the big, rugged man sitting beside a churn waiting for butter seemed about as right as snow in Texas.

He laughed. *Sure has a nice laugh. Makes me feel kind of warm inside.*

"Wouldn't that be something!" He poured more coffee into his tin cup, took another bite of eggs, and speared another slice of ham. "Miz Watkins, she's the washerwoman I told you about. She churns me butter every so often. Bakes me bread, too. These here biscuits are mighty tasty. You're about as good a baker as Miz Watkins."

Not used to compliments, Hattie kept silent. None of the gang had ever said she could bake good before. They just shoveled food in their mouths, eating, laughing, and looking like a bunch of disgusting cows chewing cud. She wanted to ask what he did for this Miz Watkins, for her to bestow so many favors, but he answered as if it was her business.

"I offer to pay her, but she won't take money; says she's just being neighborly. But a few times every week or so, she comes by to sit a spell. I read the newspaper to her. She never learned to read, but she likes to hear what's going on in the world."

Hattie, who only knew a little of her letters and had trouble reading simple words, could understand this woman's need. Only a few of the gang could read, but she listened hard when they read out loud.

The baby toddled over to lean against Hattie's leg, little rosebud mouth open – waiting.

"Now, what are you wanting?"

"Aren't you going to feed her?" Brooks asked.

"H-ho-" Hattie almost said *how*, then caught herself in time. *This here is my baby, I ought to know how to feed her.* Just then Olive grabbed the skirt of her dress and opened her mouth again.

"Look at that," Hattie grinned, "just like a little baby bird a-waiting for its mama to feed it." She chopped some egg into a mush, scooped up a spoon and dropped it in the baby's mouth. Olive chewed and swallowed, opened her mouth again. "Just like a little bird. Ain't that somethin'? Did you ever see the like?" Hattie fed Olive almost a whole egg before the baby toddled off to go stand by Brooks' leg to stare up at him with her pearly toothed grin.

"Here, she looks big enough to gnaw on a biscuit." He broke one in half and tucked it into the baby's little fist. She sat on the floor and pulled at the biscuit, putting small bites into her mouth. Even with just two teeth, she managed to gum a mush. It dribbled out the sides of her mouth.

"How old is she?" Brooks asked.

"Old?"

"Yes, when's her birthday?"

Birthday? Hattie took an extra big bite of ham to give herself time to think. Even chewing until it disappeared in her mouth, it seemed just seconds while her mind tried to ponder up an answer. "Uh – well, she was born last summer." Could that be right? Hattie grabbed a month out of thin air. "August?"

Brooks nodded as if the answer was right. "Looks to be about a year old then. I figured that with her teeth and walking. About when they start trying to get into everything too."

How did he know about babies? What they liked to eat and how old did they be? Hattie wondered but kept her mouth shut. He already knew more about babies than she did.

What secrets do you got in your life, Mister Brooks Shanton?

Suddenly, Hattie wasn't sure she wanted to know. For the first time, her heart lurched at the terror waiting in Beaumont.

Chapter Five

After they ate, Brooks built a fire in the fireplace. He pulled one of the wooden chairs in front and stretched his long legs out to the warmth. Hattie made short work of heating water, washing up the dishes, drying them off and putting them on the wooden shelves. She wiped off Olive's little hands and face.

The night had started to cool down; the fire's heat felt like a warm blanket. Hattie sat in the other wooden chair, Olive on her lap. They sat for a long while, not talking. Both of them stared into the orange and yellow flames, lost in private thoughts, listening to the crackling of the logs. Hattie felt herself nod off and jerked her head back upright. It had been a long, tiring day.

"Looks like Olive's getting tired." He nodded to the baby in her lap.

Hattie looked down, overwhelmed by a flood of feelings she couldn't name. Olive's little blonde head lay against her chest, a curled fist to her sleepy blue eyes. The solid weight and warmth of her took Hattie's breath away.

What would it be like if she really was my baby?

"Why don't you take her and put her to bed?" he said. "I'll make a pallet out here on the floor."

"No, truly, I don't mind sleeping out here. It don't seem right to just show up at your door and take your bed. Me 'n Olive can take the pallet."

He shook his head. "I'd feel better if you take the bedroom where you can close the door, in case those men come back."

"Men?"

39

"The ones who chased you," he said, giving her an odd look. Almost, Hattie thought, as if he knew straight-off no one had been chasing her.

Does he believe I've been chased? Or is he just saying that?

"You and Olive can bunk down in there."

"We wouldn't wanna put you out none. We can sleep by the fire." Hattie protested again.

"No, you take the bed. Let me get the sheets and a couple of blankets for myself."

Hattie sat by the fire, Olive a sleepy lump in her arms. Brooks came back into the front room with his arm full of blankets. "I think you've got everything you need for the night. Anything else I can help with?"

"You wouldn't have a needle and thread, so's I can mend my dress?"

"Well, um ..." Brooks gave her an uneasy glance, dropped his blankets on a chair and walked back into the bedroom. He knelt by the cedar chest and pulled open the lid. From her seat by the fire, Hattie couldn't see much of the chest's inside, just what looked like a lot of clothes and such. It took him a few minutes to hunt around, but he came back carrying a small pouch made of red velvet and tied around with black ribbons.

"Here, I think you'll find everything you need inside." His voice sounded gruff as he handed it to her. "I'm going out to check up on the animals. I'll be back in a bit. Good night."

"Good night."

Hattie didn't know if he planned to go out and drink or what. Once the door closed behind him, she carried Olive – already sound asleep – into the bedroom. Hattie laid the baby at the bottom of the bed, then took the clean sheet and smoothed it over the mattress. Olive didn't even wake up when Hattie rolled her over to smooth the sheet under her. She picked up the rumpled pink patchwork from the floor and shook it to get out the dust, disturbing a cobweb or two. She laid it gently over the sleeping baby.

"Ain't you a pretty thing," Hattie whispered, staring at the little squares of pink flowered fabric, admiring the fine, even stitches. "Wonder if that Miz Watkins sewed you?"

Hattie had never slept on such a beautiful quilt, or any quilt at all. A rough, thin army blanket was her usual blanket, a bed of pine needles as fancy as she got. Once in a great while, the gang slept in someone's house or a hotel, but Hattie hadn't often been invited inside. She could probably count on one hand the times she'd lain on a real bed.

An oil lamp sat on the dresser. Hattie found a match, lit the lamp wick, and turned the lamp so light spilled across the rocking chair.

She slipped off the torn dress and stood in the muslin petticoat. Guess she'd have to sleep in it, although it felt strange not to wear her pants and shirt. She'd brought them both in the carpetbag, but now that she thought it through, she wouldn't be able to wear them.

Hattie sat in the rocking chair and opened the velvet pouch. It was a pretty thing, too. A letter "E" embroidered in gold thread on the front. *Wonder who this belonged to?* Inside, the pouch had clever pockets with lengths of thread, a strip of felt with three sewing needles, and a pair of fancy silver scissors. They had flowers and a curvy E on the handle. Maybe the same person who owned the woman's brush and sewed the fine pink patchwork.

Wonder what it's like to own such nice things for your own. Hattie didn't know much about Brooks Shanton. Hardly anyone told her anything. Just what to do or not do. Anything she knew about him she'd learned by hearing the gang whisper.

Maybe he'd had a wife – the *E* who sewed the quilt, who used the brush and fancy sewing pouch. Maybe he'd had children ... Hattie wasn't rightly sure she wanted to know where they were now if he did.

Hattie knew Rafael wanted Brooks dead because of Mateo. She knew he'd been the sheriff in Beaumont. That he'd been nicknamed the *Golden Star,* a name Hattie thought sounded right nice – brave and true. It fit Brooks, somehow. But around the campfire she'd heard words sneered, like, "*a purveyor of truth and justice.*" Heard the snarls and the leering jests about what would happen to Brooks when he got the *justice* he deserved. Around the campfire, miles from this strange place in Louisiana, it hadn't mattered to Hattie. There were just words.

Coming here was just her job, her part in the plan.

Tonight, she thought of the man bunking by the fire, how he'd set her plate of food down before his own. Hadn't hollered or slapped when she almost dropped the biscuits. Cared if she had a bed with a clean sheet. Hattie chuckled. *Like I ever used a sheet – clean or dirty – in my life.* Having him care made her feel special, protected.

Hattie sighed. *You just mind your own business.*

It didn't take long to mend the dress.

Olive snuffled in her sleep. Hattie took a second to look at the sleeping baby. No doubt she'd wet her drawers again before morning and wake up in a wet bed, but it didn't matter. Discomfort had always been Hattie's constant companion.

Hattie sighed and crawled into the bed with the baby. The straw tick mattress crackled under her tired body, but it felt so soft. Not like sleeping on the hard ground at all. Must be fine to have comforts like this all the time.

"Oh, Olive," she whispered to the sleeping baby, "this here is fine living. Too bad it's not gonna last."

***

Brooks fixed himself a pallet on the floor in front of the fire, folding a gray blanket for a pillow. Felt strange, after so many years alone, to hear people moving around in the other room. Hattie, murmuring to Olive, the baby whimpering in her sleep and a little cough. The creak of the rocking chair on the wooden floor.

After a while, the line of light coming from under the closed door snuffed out. He heard the familiar squeak as Hattie settled into bed. Somehow, the sounds were comforting.

He'd been alone for six years now, ever since that horrible July 25th in Beaumont, when his sense of justice destroyed his whole world. Six years of silence felt too long, although until Hattie showed up at the door, he hadn't noticed it much.

Who are you, Hattie Munn?

He'd been puzzling over the question for hours. Back in Beaumont, his instincts had been as fine-tuned as a fiddle. Those barbed wires of doubt would prick his mind, and he'd sense a not-rightness about a person. Many times, it had meant the difference between life and death.

You sure aren't who you appear to be, but oh, those green eyes and that sweet, heart-shaped face. A man could drown in those eyes if he let himself ... and why should you even think such a thing? Get hold of yourself, Brooks. She's probably a wanton woman; sure not as upstanding as Emily.

Ever since her arrival at his door, he'd been skeptical about trusting Hattie at her word. The thought of a strange woman and baby showing up at his door seemed more than curious. If Hattie had come down the road, as she'd said, there were other people and houses she'd have passed first. The Overview Plantation. The Landry's. *Why pass help and come an extra two miles in the heat? With no water?*

Hattie didn't seem to know much about babies either, showing surprise at how the baby ate and being unsure about her age. He'd seen the hesitation when he asked about Olive's birthday. If the baby didn't belong to Hattie, where had she come from? A person didn't just find a baby wandering the byroads in South Louisiana.

Brooks shifted on the hard floor. Memories. Too bad some could thrust like a knife, while others were as pleasant as a woman's warm arms around him. Or a little boy sitting on the saddle in front of him ... Emily.

No, he didn't want to think about her today. There were knots in his stomach as he opened the cedar chest and saw her things again. His palms grew clammy when they touched the sewing kit her grandmother had made for her as a wedding gift. Did he just imagine it, or had the dresses she'd once worn still hold a whiff of fragrance his mind knew as Em's?

It felt strange to keep her things, to bring them all the way from Texas. Not that he didn't use some of them – the patchwork quilt on the bed, the dresser and mirror he'd had shipped from back east when she asked. The rocking chair she'd settled in to rock their boys, to sew or read...

"Don't be a darn fool," he reminded himself, breath raw in his throat. "You keep thinking like that and you'll be drowning in another bottle of whiskey."

In the morning he might see if Hattie could wear any of the dresses from the cedar chest. From his search inside the carpetbag, it didn't appear she had a change of clothes.

Brooks sighed and rolled over, trying to get comfortable, his back already feeling the pain of the wooden floor against his spine. Been a long time since he'd slept on the floor or the ground. He didn't know if Hattie's story was true or not. It grated on his mind as untrue, but strange things did happen. This was wild country, and there were banditos everywhere. He knew he still had enemies – three in particular – who would like to see him dead.

If there had been an attack on a stagecoach, the Sheriff in town would know. Time enough tomorrow to find out some answers. And maybe forget how those beguiling green eyes made his heart lurch with a pleasant feeling he hadn't known in a long, long time.

Don't be a darn fool! You don't know anything about this woman. You know better than to be fooled by a pretty face and ... Brooks smiled to himself in the dark. *She sure would be cute if she combed that hair.*

Tomorrow, he decided, as the last of the flames flickered and dropped into red coals, he would go into Houma and ask some questions. Tomorrow, he would demand the truth from Hattie, too.

He grinned to himself in the dark, she sure was a cute little thing.

Chapter Six

"I think I'd best ride into Houma this morning," Brooks announced to Hattie as she sat a plate of ham and eggs in front of him. "I'm thinking I need to talk to Sheriff Beaudry. Find out if those men tried to harm anyone else. Figure out a way to get you safely to Beaumont."

Brooks didn't share all his thoughts with Hattie. If there had been an attack on the stagecoach, the sheriff would know. If old Mr. Dupont had carried a woman and baby in the coach and they'd disappeared, people would be searching. There would be a posse out looking for them. *Strange no one had come around last night,* he'd thought during morning chores.

"Well," she looked a little doubtful at this plan, trying to get the baby to drink a tin mug of the milk Brooks had brought in earlier. The baby fretted and pushed the mug away, pursing her rosebud lips together tight and blubbering her disapproval. "I reckon the sheriff would know …"

A crease of worry crossed Hattie's forehead, he noticed. *You don't like my plan, do you?* Her eyes took on a hunted look Brooks knew well.

Olive pushed away the tin mug, sloshing milk on herself, Hattie, and the floor. A wail as the baby fretted and grabbed the skirt of Hattie's dress.

"What's wrong with her? Is she sick?"

"How am I supposed to know what's wrong?" Hattie snapped. She picked up the coffee pot and poured a stream of hot coffee into his tin mug. "She woke up peaky like that. Maybe all that sun yesterday heated her up. She didn't have no bonnet or nothin'."

Brooks touched the baby's forehead, but it didn't feel overly hot, like a fever. A rosy flush covered her cheeks, but not like it might cause pain. The baby sat on the floor, blubbering, slobbering, putting dirty fingers into her mouth, and chewing. It had been a long time, but he thought he knew the trouble.

"Could be she's getting new teeth. My boy ..." He stopped just in time from speaking names he hadn't said for the past six years. "They do like that sometimes, get all fretful and cry."

"What'm I supposed to do about it?" Hattie demanded, hands on her hips. She was showing more spirit this morning than she had yesterday.

Brooks hid a smile on his newly-shaved face. *Sure is a feisty little thing.*

"Not a whole lot you *can* do. Rubbin' her gums with clove oil could help, but I don't have any."

"You got whiskey."

"No!" Brooks didn't mean to shout, but he realized a second too late he'd startled Hattie and Olive. Olive let out a screech and buried her face in Hattie's skirt. Hattie stared hard at him, lips pressed tight. A hand reached down to touch the baby's head, and she soothed Olive with whispered shush sounds.

"You got no cause to shout," she spoke in a quiet, timid voice. "Whiskey's the only thing I know for a toothache. I seen it work."

"I'm sorry," Brooks apologized, taking a deep breath. "I can buy some clove oil when I ride into town. I was thinking we could take you and Olive into town, put you up in the hotel until we can wire your aunt and have her meet a stage. But it's more than half a day's ride, and I don't have a wagon. I've only got the one horse."

Brooks had no use for a wagon once he'd gotten his original supplies to the ranch. When he bought too many supplies he couldn't pack in on a horse and mule, a neighbor from the plantation brought them in.

"I don't know about riding so far with Olive; she's mighty fretful today," Hattie had just spoken when they heard footsteps on the front porch.

A bold knock sounded at the door. Brooks rose, grabbing the gun belt and holster from the peg beside the fireplace. He motioned Hattie to pick up the baby and go into the bedroom. Hattie did as she was told. Olive squalled like a cat.

No sense trying to hide that.

He pulled his Colt revolver out of the holster, held it ready. "Who's there?"

"Mister Brooks? S'me, John Pierre Landry."

Brooks relaxed, reupholstered the gun, and opened the door to the young Cajun boy who lived near the bayou. John Pierre, his face aglow with good cheer, wore faded overalls over a sun-bleached blue shirt and a straw hat on his dark, curly hair. As usual, his feet were bare, with callouses as hard as stone. "What brings you calling?"

"Papa went to town an' brought t'mail. You got a letter, so he told me to fet' it over to you." He handed Brooks a letter as his bright eyes searched the room. "I'm sorry I din' get down. Our boat, she sprung a leak, and we had to fix 'er."

Brooks had no trouble following the fast, clipped words spoken in John Pierre's broken Cajun English now, but during his first days in Louisiana, he had trouble understanding any of his Cajun neighbor's speech.

"Thank you and your Papa."

It's from Sam! He would recognize that old codger's hen scratch anywhere. Brooks' fingers itched to rip the envelope open and read. Politeness came first, though.

"Mister Brooks, I do' men to pry, but did I hear a baby cryin' in here j'now?"

No, can't hide a crying baby.

"Hattie," Brooks called, "come on out and meet a friend of mine."

The bedroom door opened, and Hattie walked out, carrying Olive. If the boy thought her odd, he didn't say so. His friendly grin welcomed them, and he reached up to yank off the straw hat in the presence of a lady. His brown eyes stared with curiosity at the scratches on Hattie's face.

"This here's a ... friend," Brooks explained. "Hattie and her baby, Olive. Hattie's aunt lives in Beaumont, and I offered to see she gets there. Came yesterday to surprise me. Hattie, this is John Pierre Landry. His family lives in the bayou nearby, run a fishing business. They do neighborly things for me, bring my mail ..." He held up the letter, eager to open it but too polite to read it right then.

"*Ça c'est bon!*" John Pierre's grin lit his whole face in a smile. "Pleased to meet you, Ma'am. Mighty cute bébé."

It was nice of him to say that, even as Olive began screeching like a banshee.

The boy looked startled. "Why she fret?"

"She's cutting new teeth," Brooks explained. He didn't mind John Pierre knowing Hattie and the baby were here – much. But he knew once John Pierre went home and told his Mama, Miz Landry would pass on the news to near and far. Brooks couldn't say why, but the less people who knew about Hattie, the better.

"Oh!" The boy grinned in understanding. "*Maman* use oil of clove on my brudda's tee'."

"Would she have some she could spare?" Hattie asked, the first time she'd spoken since John Pierre's knock. "I don't like to ask for no favors, but I don't like to see her suffering."

"People in Louisiana," John Pierre spoke, pronouncing it *Lesanna* as most of the Cajuns did, "don' mind doing favors. If *Maman* knew, she be hurt you din' let her help. I will run right home and ask."

Brooks knew John Pierre well enough to know he loved to do favors. Favors took time away from having to catch crawfish or sail his Papa's boat into Houma where the well-to-do bought fish from his family.

"Thank you for bringing my letter," Brooks told him.

"Most welcome," John Pierre said, slapping the straw hat back over his dark hair, his brown eyes shining. "I will run like the wind an' brin' back the medicine for the bébé."

Once John Pierre had jumped off the porch, scattered the hens pecking around the yard, and taken off out of sight, Brooks shut the door.

"I didn't like him knowing you were here," Brooks said, "but with Olive crying, I figured it was best to be open."

"Weren't nothing you could do," she agreed, joggling Olive on her hip, the baby fretting and whining. "Hope he can bring some clove oil for her teeth. I'm about wore out walkin' this floor. He sure do talk funny, don't he? Couldn't rightly understand most of his words, the way he sliced them all apart and talked so fast."

Eager to get away from her prying eyes, Brooks took time to explain the boy's lilting speech. "He's Cajun. They speak a kind of French-Canadian – well – I guess I'm used to how he talks.

"It shouldn't take him long." Brooks itched to read Sam's letter. "Why don't you walk out to the corral and show Olive the calf? Maybe get her mind off her teeth?"

Hattie nodded, glancing back as Brooks slit the envelope and drew out a single sheet of paper. He waited until she and Olive had gone into the barn before he read the note before him. The words were written by his old deputy, Sam Rathbone.

Dear Brooks,

How you been? Sorry I'm such a poor hand at keeping in touch. Just wanted to ask you a favor and hope you'll do it. Wanted you to hear it from me. They're back and planning on taking over where Mateo left off. People are scared. The town is riled, and things is going to come to a bad end unless we do something. Mateo was cruel – you remember how vicious. The rest of them are even worse. They're ruthless. You know how bad they can be.

Michael's a good enough Sheriff, but he's young. He's never had to deal with the likes of the Avila gang. Sure hate to ask but can you come back and help me round them up? I know you won't want to. I know you shook the dust of this town off your boots six years ago. But, Brooks, you were the best Sheriff Beaumont ever had. We need you back. Beaumont needs the Golden Star.

You can stay at my ranch. The latch string is always out for you – just like it always was when you lived here. Sam

A short letter, but it took Brooks' breath away.

Mateo. The very memory chilled his blood. How many times had he woken from a restless sleep, screaming in remembered terror of the brutality, the killing, the maiming, the horror Mateo and his gang had inflicted on Beaumont for too long?

It wasn't hard to recall the gut-wrenching day he'd watched Mateo twist from the end of a rope. Watched the bandito cursing and fighting his way up the gallows steps. Clenched his jaw as a hangman's rope – a justified rope – snuffed out Mateo's life. Justice had been done that day ... or so Brooks thought. Now Sam wanted him to come back to Beaumont. To face the three men who had destroyed his life six years ago.

Sam needed him, had asked for him. But what would happen if he went back to Beaumont? It might be easier to just jump off a cliff instead of facing those demons again.

Brooks drew in a deep, ragged breath. *I can't, Sam. I just can't.*

Chapter Seven

"See the pretty little cow?" Hattie jiggled Olive up and down outside the corral fence, where a calf stared at them with huge, brown eyes. Another cow stood to the side, chewing cud, eyeing them with protective intensity. The baby stopped crying for half a second, looked at the calf, then went to blubbering again.

"I'm sorry, baby. Maybe that John Pierre boy will come back soon. Is your little mouth hurtin?"

Hattie stared back at the porch, watching as Brooks read the letter. Sure would be fine if she knew what it said. A few days before, she'd overheard Rafael tell Francisco that there was only one way to get Brooks Shanton back to Texas. Although she hadn't heard all their talk, she did hear Rafael say something about a letter. Making someone write a letter. *Was that it?*

'Course what he whispered was, *"Hold a knife to his throat and make him write what I say."*

"Wonder what he's reading?" She asked Olive and turned to see the baby toddling after the chickens. "Olive, you come back here, now!"

The hens were having none of those baby fingers grabbing their tail feathers. The flock scattered and squawked, going in a dozen different directions on their skinny chicken feet. Olive thought this was great fun. Her chubby legs chased after first one hen, then another. A rooster squawked and flew up to the corral fence.

Oh well, at least she forgot about her mouth hurting.

Hattie leaned back against the corral fence, the sun burning down on her head, wishing she dared wear her sombrero.

Even if Brooks laid the paper down and she picked it up, Hattie wouldn't be able to read the letter. She knew her letters – at least the print kind – scratched out in the dirt by Francisco. There were a few words she could read, but the swirly kind of writing was just ink on paper.

Staring at the cabin, she watched Brooks. The big man seemed to shrink as he crumpled the letter in one hand. A few minutes later, he went into the cabin and shut the door. An odd sensation plucked at Hattie's heart, like maybe she should comfort him. Hattie stayed by the fence as a memory came back to haunt her, another time when her hard heart had melted, and she wanted to comfort someone.

It wasn't a memory Hattie liked to recall – the terror on the woman's face, the husband writhing on the ground, their three little children, standing there still as stone.

The gang had taken the family's flour, cornmeal, coffee, and sugar, then ransacked the barn for livestock. They'd done it dozens of times before. When they needed to eat, Mateo or Rafael had no problem helping himself from someone else's homestead.

It wasn't often Hattie could look around people's homes, see how they lived. She couldn't imagine having real furniture and fine things; she'd learned early on that anything she cherished could be crushed under someone's boot in an instant.

In this farmhouse, her eyes were riveted to a wooden cabinet. The prettiest dishes she'd ever seen sat in little grooves that stood them up, not stacked like anybody else's plates. The elegant China was painted with a rosebud design, and something about those clean, shiny dishes, near about took Hattie's breath away.

"What's that there thing called?" she'd asked.

Francisco, hands all sticky from the apple pie he'd stolen from a windowsill, had guessed, "El *armario* – a cupboard?" But it didn't look like an ordinary cupboard. It must have a fancier name. Hattie wasn't often given to flights of fancy, but at that moment, she thought, *someday I'll have a fine house with a cupboard like that.*

Rafael began a game. "Let's see how many of the *gringo*'s dishes we can shoot!"

Pressing her lips tight, Hattie said nothing as the shots rang out. She forced herself not to recoil each time a dish shattered or another hole punctured the walnut back of the cabinet. Each bullet wrenched Hattie's heart, but she said nothing.

Weren't *no call to smash 'em just 'cause a person could.*

It was best not to question Rafael. Ever. Somehow, none of the gang noticed the teapot sitting in the sink. Hattie stared at it for the longest time. The small lid on top had a glass violet to lift it open. She stared outside at the woman, kneading her hands in that yellow apron, and wondered how it would be to make tea and lift the violet lid.

Hattie thought of trying to take the teapot but knew it would be shattered before they got back to camp.

Hattie had never allowed herself to care about anyone else. Wasn't no stake in that. But at that moment, she knew with all her heart no one was going to shoot that teapot. While the others were laughing, stumbling around, tossing muddy boots to the top of an ornate walnut table, and scratching it with their spurs, Hattie took a chance.

A bowl of potato peelings sat on the dry sink. Moving as quiet as a snake, she tipped it over on top of the teapot. Then she nudged a dirty towel over the whole mess. Maybe the woman would find it later and know someone had cared about her pretty teapot. At that moment, Hattie couldn't have said why she cared. *Maybe finding her teapot will bring the woman some comfort when she looks at all this mess.*

Later, driving a wagonload of stolen supplies, Hattie heard the gunshots and her heart clenched as those tormented faces came to mind. No one would ever find the teapot anyway – not until someone came to claim the bodies. Rafael would've made sure of that.

Hattie's stomach tightened, and she hardened her heart – or tried to. This time it was more difficult than it usually was. *Why? Just because Brooks gave you sheets for a bed. Just because he gave you food and didn't try to touch you …*

Don't be fooled. Don't go soft now. Except, there was the strangest warm feeling around her heart when Brooks' face came to mind. What would it be like to run her hand over that rugged jaw, to brush that fine chestnut hair off his forehead? *To touch a man like a woman ought to.*

Pretty soon now, Shanton would be a dead man, just like that family at the farm.

Why, Hattie wondered, *do you care?*

Chapter Eight

After waiting a while, Hattie herded Olive away from the hens and went into the cabin.

Brooks sat at the kitchen table, the letter nowhere in sight. "Why did you come here, Hattie?"

The question startled her. Hattie sat Olive down and watched her toddle off.

Brooks sat there, staring at her.

"I told you," she stammered, "men chased me. I ran for my life."

Her heart beat so hard under the green calico bodice, she thought it might burst out. *What does he know? Or suspect? And what's Rafael gonna do about this? What's gonna happen to me when he knows I failed?*

The thought didn't bear thinking. Hattie's body quivered at what might come, eyes haunted with an inner pain.

"Yes, I remember what you told me," he said, kind of sad-like. Shifting in the chair, his next words were unexpected. "That letter I got today was from an old friend, Sam. He used to be my deputy when I lived in Beaumont. He's asked me to come back, stay at his ranch, help him with something I should have done too long ago."

Hattie waited, not sure what to say.

"I've decided," Brooks said, "since you and Olive were on your way to Beaumont anyway to stay with your aunt ..."

He paused, as if he didn't quite believe that part, then continued. "I'm going to take you with me. I can see you safely there. That way you won't have to worry about being accosted again. We can ride into Houma and take the stage to Beaumont."

"Oh!" The word passed her lips in a surprised exclamation, then her expression shifted from nervous to relieved. "I surely do appreciate that. Only, what about money? Those men took my money; I ain't got no way to pay the fare."

He waved off her concerns. "No need to worry. I can pay your fare. And your ..." Why did he hesitate? "... *aunt* can pay me back when we get there. I'll borrow a horse from one of my neighbors and hire someone to take care of my ranch while I'm gone."

"All right, if you think it best. I surely would welcome the company." *And Rafael can't say I failed, not if I bring you back to Beaumont.*

"You'll be wanting something else to wear. If you can find anything in the cedar chest that fits, you're welcome to take it. There are some dresses, and ..." His voice trailed off, heavy and sad.

Olive began to whimper from the bedroom.

"We'll leave in the morning."

Morning! Tomorrow, Rafael's dust-devil plan will spin off in the right direction. He'll get his way with Brooks' return.

Hattie hardened her heart to what would happen in Beaumont.

Not no never-mind of mine. I'm just doing what I'm told. Except ...

A sick feeling stole over her. Sure would be a sorrowful thing if Rafael hurt Brooks like he planned. *He's a nice man, an honest man. What did he ever do to Rafael?*

Before she went to bed that night, Hattie searched through the cedar chest, holding up first one and then another beautiful dress. There were four altogether: dark blue, faded yellow with purple violets in the print, dark red with splotches like blackberries, and satin with lace and fine tucks across the bodice. The last didn't look to be serviceable enough to ride saddle in but, oh, how fine! Hattie smoothed the silkiness of it against her sunburnt cheek. Reluctantly, she folded it back in the trunk.

Hattie held the other dresses up to her chest and studied herself in the dresser mirror. Funny, she'd never thought about dressing like any other woman in pretty furbelows. Her trousers and shirt were good enough for her. They were her protection, her cover from anyone thinking she was a girl. When people knew she was a girl, there was always trouble.

Wonder who wore these clothes before? Where is she now?

Hattie laid the dresses back in the chest and rummaged around. There were a few little boy's clothes – linen shirts and well-worn pants. A well-loved wooden train and a little ball made from string. Strange keepsakes for Brooks to have. Again, she wondered about this man she'd met. *Who is he?*

Olive moaned in her sleep. Quickly, before the baby woke up, Hattie grabbed the dark blue dress and laid it over the rocking chair. She blew out the lamp and got into bed, dreading what tomorrow might bring. Despite her worry, a faint smile crossed her lips. Would Brooks think she looked pretty in the blue dress?

***

Brooks rose early the next day, did the chores, saddled the horses, and packed up a satchel for himself. Hattie had fixed breakfast, washed up the dishes and packed her carpetbag.

At his suggestion, she'd boiled some eggs and made extra biscuits to take along for lunch.

"It's going to be late afternoon when we get to Houma," he told her. "We'll want to eat along the way."

The sight of Hattie in Emily's dark blue dress with the lace collar tore his heart in two. He tried not to let his thoughts linger too long on his feelings. Taking Hattie into Houma in that mended green calico would be sure to raise questions. Having her and Olive along was going to raise enough eyebrows as it was. Hattie needed to look like a respectable woman, a friend sent for him to squire to Beaumont. He wondered if it could be that simple, and he wrestled a knot of worry all through their preparations.

If Hattie is who she pretends to be, am I dragging her and the baby into danger? What if the gang attacks as we get to Beaumont? Can I protect them? Surely when he got to Sam's ranch they could figure it out together. *Sam will know what to do.*

When the sun began to rise, they were packed and ready to set out. Brooks hadn't thought to ask if Hattie could ride; he'd just assumed. It surprised him to see her pull herself into the saddle, riding just like a man, although she had to bunch up the skirt of the blue dress to her knees. Emily had always ridden astride too – but she'd had a riding skirt. It appeared Hattie planned to ride in the long dress the best she could.

Brooks averted his eyes from the bare skin between her unmentionables and stockinged leg hanging down to the stirrups. At least her boots looked sturdy enough. Worn and old, but serviceable for the trip. Strangely enough, she had pulled the old sombrero from the carpet bag and clapped it on her head. When she noticed him looking at it, her lips pressed in a tight line. A *don't-mess-with-me* look. Inside, he wanted to chuckle at the face, but he kept it to a slight upwards curve of his lips.

Maybe I need to smile at a woman more often. Funny, how it lifts my heart. Strange how having a woman around again makes me feel kind of – kind of strange. Brooks reined in his heart, pressed his lips tight. *You just feel sorry for her is all. You can't be starting to have* feelings *for some girl you just met a day ago!*

"Can you hand me up the baby?" she asked once she'd gotten settled in the saddle, carpetbag hanging from the pommel.

"Here you go, Olive." He lifted the baby up to sit on Hattie's lap in the saddle.

Olive stared around, her eyes big *O*'s, as if unsure of this adventure.

"Doesn't look like she's ever been on a horse before," Brooks said, realizing he hadn't thought about that either. *Maybe I should have asked Mister Overview to borrow the use of a wagon. Just because my boys were born to the saddle doesn't mean every baby takes to it right off.*

"It don't matter," Hattie said. "She's gonna be okay." As he watched, Hattie pulled the edge of her reins and put it in Olive's hand. Olive, unsure at first, lifted the reins to her mouth and chewed. A big grin crossed her face. Maybe it felt cool on her sore gums. John Pierre had returned yesterday with the clove oil and Olive seemed to be fit to travel this morning.

Brooks pulled himself into Midnight's saddle. "I guess we're ready, then."

He tried not to look back as they took the road leading away from the cabin. Tried not to anticipate whatever lay in store.

"Brooks," Pa had advised long ago, *"when you face trouble, you got two choices. Turn and run like a coward, or make your mind as hard as those steel railroad ties and don't look back."*

The ride into Houma was long, tiring, and hot. The sun rose in the East and took its sweet time rolling across the sky, beating down in unrelenting rays. Sweat trickled down his scalp, and Brooks was grateful for his wide-brimmed hat. Every little while, he took the hat off, swiped a bandana over his head and put it back on. Hattie seemed to be cool enough beneath that ragged sombrero. Thankfully, she'd tied the sunbonnet over Olive's fair hair to protect her baby-white cheeks.

As they rode along, Brooks reached into his shirt pocket and pulled out his old badge. He still treasured it. It was the only badge he knew made from solid gold, a gift from his thankful community.

"What's that you got there?" Hattie asked from behind him. The trail made it impossible to ride side by side, so the horses had been following one another for the last few miles.

Brooks held it over his shoulder, the six-pointed star gleaming in the sun. "It's my badge, from when I was sheriff. I've kept it ever since ..." He stopped, swallowing past the memories. "Ever since I left. I took great pride in being a sheriff. It's all I ever wanted to do in life."

"It's right pretty."

He anticipated her next question and wasn't disappointed. "So how come you quit being sheriff?"

"It's a long story," he said, shifting in the saddle. Midnight's hooves sent up puffs of dust with every step. "Ever since I was knee-high, I'd wanted to be a sheriff. The best sheriff Beaumont ever had. The law is a good thing, Hattie. It's the difference between–" His face grew warm as he spoke the words, knowing they might sound preachy to someone like the girl behind him. "The law is the difference between good and evil. That's my thought, anyway. Some people work hard, build up their farms and ranches. They live good lives, and they should keep what they earn with their hands. That side's the good – good people, good lives, never bother nobody else."

"Da da, ba, ba," Olive chortled from behind him. No word from Hattie.

Taking a deep breath, trying to put his thoughts into words, Brooks went on. "Then there's the bad. People like the Avila gang." A gasp sounded behind him but when he turned his head to glance at Hattie, she seemed to be fixing Olive's sunbonnet, eyes downcast.

"Gangs, banditos, they're the bad in the world. They cheat, steal, kill, maim. They take the good lives away from people for themselves. That's where the law comes in. People make laws so the good keep their lives and the bad get just rewards. Like hanging or jail."

"Maybe," she said in a timid voice, "maybe some folks think people shouldn't get hung for taking food and stuff ... if they're hungry."

"People who get hung usually deserve it, Hattie. That's justice, and justice is what keeps us all from becoming like a pack of ravenous wolves, taking what we want with no regard for anybody else. People aren't animals. If folks are really hungry, they can work on growing their own food or find work."

They rode another few hours before they stopped, around noon, near a small stream. While Brooks led the horses to water, then tied their reins to a branch, Hattie let Olive down to toddle around. She pulled out the saddlebag of boiled eggs, ham, and biscuits, and fed the baby with a distracted air, as if she might be thinking deep thoughts.

"We'll rest here a bit," Brooks said after they'd eaten. "Looks like Olive is ready to take a nap."

The baby had curled up in Hattie's lap. Brooks laid down on a grassy mound, covered his face with the wide-brimmed hat, and dozed.

***

Hattie stared down at Olive's sweet baby-face in her lap, her long dark lashes against her cheeks, those little rosebud lips pursed like she might be fixing to start singing. A smile curved her own lips.

What would it be like to have a baby for my own?

A gentle snore came from under Brooks' hat. Hattie chuckled, spreading out the skirt of the dark blue dress under her hands. It felt so fine, so soft. She'd noticed too how Brooks took one glance at her in it and tried not to look again. *He's missing the woman who wore this before. What would it be like to have a man think of me as a woman – a real woman – and get that look at missing me?*

The baby chuckled in her sleep, snuggling tighter into Hattie's lap. The solid little weight of her was warm and comforting. Spending the long day yesterday with Olive – a burden to be sure – had been hard. Trying to keep her fed, give her water – it felt like a bothersome chore to be endured. Today, staring down into that sweet baby-face, something stirred in Hattie's heart – like holding the little rabbit.

For the first time in a long time, Hattie thought about the baby rabbit. She tried not to remember such things – to be hard and not soft – but the rabbit had hurt so awful bad. It was, maybe, the last time she let caring rip her heart out.

Once, right after she'd been sold to the gang, she'd found a little gray rabbit caught in a bear trap. It squealed in pain, brown eyes terrified, struggling to get out. Hattie had been alone, gathering firewood, her legs stinging like fire from a recent whipping. Alone, she'd let tears fall for her own sorry state, but seeing the rabbit, she forgot her own pain.

Hattie dropped the wood, pulling and yanking until the trap sprung open. Even though it was a wild creature, it just stared up at her with trusting brown eyes, not scared or anything. *Or maybe,* she'd thought later, *it knew it wasn't going to live long.*

She cradled it up in her arms, feeling its little heart go *pittypat pittypat* against her chest. The gang had been off somewhere, so she took it back to camp and hid it in her tent. Later, once she'd built up the fire and got a stew going, she'd cleaned its wound and tied a rag around the bloody leg.

Hattie hadn't thought ahead to how she'd keep a pet, keep it a secret. It didn't matter just then. That night, she slept with the rabbit curled against her chest. Its warm, soft little body brought comfort instead of the scared, alone feeling she usually had at night. It snuggled next to her as her heart stirred strangely.

When she woke the next morning, the rabbit's body was stiff and cold. It had died in the night. Hattie felt tears come, but choked them back and got up.

Her thought was to bury the little thing, but Edmundo, Mateo's cousin, found it and shouted to the others. "Hattie found us a rabbit for our supper tonight."

She couldn't watch them skin and cut up the rabbit or put the meat into the stew. At supper, she ate the stew; she knew if she showed weakness she would be beaten or ridiculed. Later, after she ate, she went into the woods and her guts turned inside out.

Remembering hurt as bad as any whipping or vile names, to know she'd held that little rabbit against her chest, alive and counting on her. She told herself it was good the rabbit had died. She could see some of them snatching it up and killing it in front of her. Hattie liked rabbit stew, she'd eaten enough of it ... but those rabbits were game, meat – not one she'd held and cuddled in her arms.

Two days ago, taking Olive had just felt like following orders. Today, it felt wrong.

While Brooks and Olive slept, Hattie stared off at the trees and thought long and hard. Brooks' words came back to haunt her. "*Good people, good lives, never bother nobody else.*" What would it be like to live like good people? Maybe like the woman who would never use her teapot with the violet on the lid again? Or like the woman who had worn this blue dress and used the velvet sewing kit?

Hattie had never been one to question the choices she made. *Don't rightly figure I've ever had any choices.* Her only choice was to either do what the gang said straightaway or get beaten, then do what they said.

Is it too late for me to change my life? To be like good people?

It was such an enormous thought, Hattie held her breath at the very idea.

If I did, how long would I live until Rafael found me?

Chapter Nine

It was around suppertime when they arrived in the bustling town of Houma; both adults were saddle sore, but Brooks was surprised at how well Olive stood the trip. They'd taken turns holding her on their saddles. Now, Olive's tiny fists rubbed her eyes, drowsy with sleep.

Once they reached the edge of town, Hattie grew as skittish as a newborn colt and quickly changed the sombrero for the sunbonnet. Eyes downcast, she rode behind him silently, avoiding friendly nods or smiles. She kept her face ducked down in the sunbonnet, like a turtle hiding in its shell.

"Hi, Brooks!"

"How do, Mister Shanton!"

Brooks' friends and neighbors called out as they rode by. He nodded, tipped his hat to the ladies, only too aware of the questioning glances at Hattie and Olive. *Curious as cats, every one of them.*

Brooks arranged to leave the horses at the livery. It took a bit of fancy word twisting to sidestep chatty Mr. McNally and his endless questions. It wasn't every day Brooks showed up with a young woman and baby in tow, and Brooks could only imagine the gossip going on behind his back. He answered the livery owner as briefly as possible, telling him that Hattie was a friend he'd offered to chaperone to Beaumont. The man's inquisitive brown eyes stared through the answer with suspicion.

"Sure enough?" Mr. McNally asked, as if he wanted to question more. "Right nice of you, Brooks."

Brooks was glad to escape the man's interrogation and join Hattie on the boardwalk.

"Would you like to eat supper at the café?" Brooks asked, satisfied the horses were settled in stalls with fresh straw and grain.

Hattie stood awkwardly beside him, Olive pressed tight to her chest. She shielded the baby's face from anyone who seemed to be staring with curiosity in their eyes. "I reckon me and Olive can just finish up what we brought from your house."

"Don't be silly, we can have a hot meal."

"I'm right tired; maybe you could bring me something," Hattie suggested. "Once we figure out where we're going to sleep. You plan to pitch a tent outside of town? Or someone got a barn we can sleep in?"

"We'll stay in the hotel," Brooks answered and led the way to the Cattleman's Hotel. Did he just imagine it, or did Hattie hold back, shielding Olive's face against her dress? *Why is she so afraid?* While Hattie waited on a plush green divan in the lobby, Brooks paid for two hotel rooms: one for Hattie and Olive, and one for himself. He could see Hattie's relief when he unlocked her hotel room and handed her the key.

"This is right fine," she said, green eyes sparkling like an excited little girl as she sat a sleepy Olive on the freshly made bed. "Sure beats sleeping on the ground."

He left her there, opening drawers in the dresser and the wardrobe, exploring the room as if she were Olive's age. Before he closed the door, she sat on the bed and bounced Olive up and down. A grin rewarded him. "Nice and soft."

Brooks went to the café alone but had dinner with the Sheriff of Houma, Ken Beaudry. Before he sat down at a table with a red-checked cover, he ordered a meal sent up to Hattie and Olive. It gave him time to talk to Ken. Brooks didn't come right out and repeat Hattie's tale, just asked a few questions to see if Ken could shed some light on the story.

"Had any trouble around here lately? Any problems with the stagecoach?"

A dark-haired waitress in a long black dress covered with a freshly-ironed white apron sat steaming plates of food before them. "I'll be back to freshen yoor coffee," she said in a lilting Irish accent, straightening a small wrinkle in the tablecloth and moving a basket of bread slices closer to the center of the table. "We've a grand peach cobbler if ye gents want some sweet when ye finish eatin'."

"Thanks, Katie, I might take you up on that." The girl smiled and hurried back to the kitchen.

"What was that you asked, Brooks? Trouble? Not so's I heard," Sheriff Beaudry answered, picking up a knife and fork. He sliced a bite of roast beef, scooped up a mound of mashed potatoes covered in thick gravy and shoveled it all into his mouth. After a few moments of chewing, he continued. "Spoke to Old Mac after his last mail run on Tuesday. Said he had a good trip, except one of the horses threw a shoe near Riverton Station. Had to waste three or four hours until the blacksmith got it fixed. Any reason for asking?"

"No." Brooks sampled a tasty bite of beef. "Just wondering. Someone out my way mentioned they heard there might have been trouble."

"Not so's I heard," Ken repeated, reaching for the salt cellar and sprinkling salt liberally over his potatoes. "Town's been quiet, except for Ben Campbell getting drunk and smashing the window in Murdoch's Saloon. That's why I took this job as Sheriff – not much ever happens. Suits me fine."

Brooks laughed.

"Saw you ride in with a woman and a baby. Any relation?"

Stalling for time, Brooks reached for a slice of bread, still warm from the oven, and spread it liberally with butter. "Not as such; I offered to see her safely to Beaumont. Not safe for a woman traveling alone."

Ken looked as if that answer didn't satisfy him, but shrugged as if it were none of his business. "Sounds like you, Brooks, always helping someone else out. Well, wish you a safe journey."

They finished the meal and ended with peach cobbler.

Okay, Hattie, so you weren't attacked by men on a stagecoach? Where did you come from?

***

Early the next morning, Brooks bought two fares to Beaumont on the 9:00 o'clock stage. Hattie had hidden in her room, again refusing to eat breakfast at the café. When she came out, worn satchel in hand, she chewed nervously on her lip. As they waited on the boardwalk in front of the stage office, she stared with suspicion at everyone who passed.

"This all, folks?" asked the stage driver, a red-haired man Brooks had never met. His freckled face and twinkling hazel eyes welcomed them as he tossed Hattie's worn satchel and Brooks' saddlebags up on top of the stage. "Mighty cute little gal there." He chucked Olive under the chin and held open the coach's door for them to climb inside. "All in? Then we're on our way!"

The trip was long, hot, and tiring. Brooks would've rather gone the distance in a saddle than endure the stage's jolts and bounces over the rough, rocky road, but the stage was easier for Hattie and Olive. Two hundred and forty miles was a long way to travel in the saddle. There was also the fact that

Sam's letter had sounded urgent. Going by stage would be faster.

Thankfully, they were the only passengers except for a drummer, a man who sold buttons and pins and seemed disinclined to talk. He stared out the open window and kept to himself, disembarking half a day from Houma. They had the stage to themselves the rest of the way. At the Kingston Station, while they waited for fresh horses to be hitched to the wagon, Hattie ventured to ask, "What are you gonna do with me when we get to Beaumont?"

What a strange question. "Take you to meet your aunt, of course," he answered, startled by the odd expression that crossed her face.

"Oh," she said in a quiet voice.

Unless there isn't an aunt waiting. Now that he'd spoken to Sheriff Casey, Brooks again felt those barbed wires of doubt.

Why did you show up at my door? Why did you lie about being attacked by men? Where did you come from? And why do I keep thinking about how fetching you look in Emily's blue dress?

"Or ..." he continued nonchalantly, staring off at the stage driver who had stopped to pull up a dipperful of water from the well, anywhere but the hopeful expression on Hattie's face. "I've been thinking. If we have trouble finding your aunt, maybe you can stay at Sam's ranch for a while with Olive. He wouldn't mind. There's a woman there who keeps house and her husband takes care of the stock. We wouldn't be there alone. It might be best, until we get you settled."

Hattie's relief, a sparkle in those green eyes, convinced him he'd made the right decision. "That might be best. Auntie's getting on in years. She might have forgot I'm coming."

"You'll stay at the ranch a few days then." *Right where I can watch you and figure this out.*

Now, why do I feel so glad about having you around a while longer?

The stage would have carried them all the way into Beaumont, but Brooks knew they didn't need to travel the twenty miles into town and then back to Sam's ranch. If they got off earlier, at the last way station, it was an easy five-mile ride to Sam's. "Do you mind if we go straight to the ranch?" he asked Hattie as she lifted Olive down so the baby could stretch her legs. "I'm going to ask if we can borrow a horse and buggy so we can ride on to Sam's." He didn't mention the urgency he felt to get there. "We can figure out how to get in touch with your aunt later."

Come quickly, Sam had written.

"Sure enough," Hattie answered fast, almost too agreeable, "that sounds fine." Almost like she'd dreaded the trip into town. "If you're sure your friend will welcome the company."

"It's a big ranch and Sam will be glad to see the baby," Brooks said, then went to talk to the station master about the horse and wagon.

"Why, sure, Brooks," Ambrose Gains, the station master, agreed. A laugh jiggled his white-bearded face and his blue eyes twinkled. "I've known you and Sam for years. Reckon if I can't trust our old Sheriff and his deputy to return my horse and wagon, there's no trusting anyone. I'll let you take Jim, my old saddle horse; he's slow enough he won't jostle the ladies too much. Give me a few minutes to help the stage driver get a hot meal and I'll help you with the wagon."

It took more than a few minutes to hitch up the rugged wooden wagon; Brooks felt impatient as the minutes ticked by, but finally he was able to lift Hattie and Olive up to the spring seat and climb on himself. He was unsure why he was so anxious to get to Sam's, but the drive over the familiar dusty road stretched like a hundred miles instead of five.

The house looked just as Brooks remembered: a sprawling, two-story *hacienda* with beige stucco walls and red clay roof dozing in the sun. Sam's ranch was surrounded by acres of corral fence, a huge barn, and a small cabin toward the back that belonged to the couple who worked for him. Smoke curled from the chimney of the Jackson cabin, but Sam's house was still and silent. Brooks pulled on the reins, "Whoa, Jim!" Forgetting his gentlemanly manners, he jumped off the wagon, leaving Hattie to climb off on her own. Brooks raced up the porch steps and knocked on the door.

"Sam! I'm here!"

Silence. The windmill creaked near the well and a horse lifted its head over the corral fence to whinny a welcome, but all other sounds were muted. He opened the sturdy log door and called inside. "Sam!"

Hattie came to stand beside him, Olive in her arms. "Maybe he's not home."

"Maybe not," Brooks agreed, "but he'll be back soon, I'm sure. He won't mind if we make ourselves at home." He held the door wide for her, reaching out to take Olive in his arms. "I'm sure Miss Olive is tired of riding, aren't you, little lady?"

As the baby reached up to pat the side of his face, Brooks paused for a moment on the porch. Two wooden rocking chairs creaked back and forth in a slight breeze. They brought back memories of sitting out here with Sam, their booted feet lifted to the wide railing that skirted the porch.

We used to talk for hours about how we'd clean up Beaumont. How we'd rid the town of the Avila gang. Sure was fine talk, wasn't it Sam? As soon as we captured two of them, I turned my tail and ran off, leaving you to find the other three. All because of what they did to Emily and the boys.

"Is it too late?"

He didn't realize he'd spoken out loud until Hattie asked, "Too late for what?"

"Nothing ... just thinking." *Remembering the happy times we spent here with Sam – me, Emily, and our boys. Is it too late to find that kind of happiness again?*

A damp Olive wiggled to be let down. As he sat her on her feet, he heard Sam's letter crinkle in his breast pocket. *Sam asked me for a reason, a desperate reason.*

Where are you, Sam?

Chapter Ten

"Mister Brooks!" Brooks turned to watch as a dark-skinned woman, dressed in a loose green shirt and a long beige skirt covered with a black apron hurried from the cabin. "You came!"

"Mavi!"

The woman scurried up the porch, lifting the skirt to reveal calloused bare feet. Her dark eyes shone with relief and a sunny smile of welcome.

"Oh, Mister Brooks, I'm mighty glad you're here! Mighty glad."

Brooks grasped her outstretched hands and clasped them. "It's so good to see you again, Mavi. Been too long."

"You're right about that," she said, holding tight to his hands, and he felt a slight tremor shudder through her body. *Mavi, afraid?* Before Brooks could question her, Mavi turned to eye Hattie with unveiled curiosity.

"Oh, Mavi, this is a friend, Hattie Munn, and her baby, Olive. Sam invited her to stay on here awhile," he lied. "Until I can take her on to Beaumont to meet her aunt."

Later, I will tell Mavi the truth about Hattie. See if she has any ideas.

"That so? Who might your aunt be?" Mavi dropped Brooks' hands and turned to Hattie, staring her up and down, noticing, Brooks thought, the healing scratches on her cheeks, the short blonde hair, Hattie's obvious discomfort at being there. Nothing would escape Mavi's notice. She would be sure to question him later, he knew.

"Hattie Munn," Hattie murmured, spooked by Mavi's intense gaze.

"Munn, Munn, don't reckon as I've ever heard her mentioned before. She lived around here long?"

"Two years," Hattie mumbled, ducking her face back in the sunbonnet's folds, as if she wanted to hide from Mavi's scrutiny.

The woman stared hard at Hattie. "Hm ..." Mavi's mouth opened as if she wanted to say something, but then changed her mind. "Well, I sure don't get to town much and I sure don't hang around the white folks either. So, the name doesn't sound familiar." She turned back to Brooks. "Y'all must be hungry. Let me fix you somethin' to eat?"

"In a minute, Mavi. Where's Sam?"

A worried frown creased her lips, her forehead furrowing with lines. Mavi twisted capable hands in the black apron. "I don't rightly know, Mister Brooks. When I saw you ride in, I was hopin' you'd come to tell me. He been gone for a while now. Me and Jed, we're gettin' worried. I sent Jed into town a few days ago, but no one seen Mister Sam."

"Jed is Mavi's husband," Brooks explained to Hattie. He turned back to Mavi, concern for Sam making him sound harsher than he meant to. "Did Jed speak to Sheriff Storey?"

A nod. "Yes sir, he done that first thing. Sheriff Storey said he worried too. Said he'd planned to come ask if *we* knew anything."

"You don't know where he went? What he planned to do?"

"No, sir, and that's the strange thing." Mavi twisted the apron tight, her voice shaky with fear. "He rode off one mornin' for town, just like always. Said he'd probably stay at the jail a couple days before he came on home. Told me and Jed what needed to be done here, and that's the last we seen of him."

"When was that?"

"Near about two weeks ago."

Two weeks. Strange that Sam would be gone for so long.

An uneasy tremor passed through Brooks' body, and he clenched his hands at his side. *Where are you, Sam? What's happened to you?*

Noticing Mavi staring at him for reassurance, Brooks managed a casual smile. "Well, you know Sam. He probably set off to do one thing and ended up going fishing or something else. I'll go into town soon and talk to Michael. Maybe he's heard something about Sam by now."

Now isn't the time to tell her about Sam's letter.

Mavi managed a trembling smile, but not as if she believed him. "If he's off fishin', I'd be right glad to know he's all right, but he's sure enough gonna get a scolding when he comes home. Now let me fix you all some supper. You're rightly half-starved and that baby look like she could use a biscuit or two."

Brooks glanced down at Olive, who was clenching his pant leg. Her blue eyes stared in frank curiosity at Mavi, as if she'd never seen anyone with dark skin before. He reached down and picked her up. "Are you hungry, Miss Olive?"

The baby chuckled and pulled at his hat. It tilted down, covering his eyes. A rush of emotions surged through his heart and a prickle of tears moistened his eyes.

My George and James did the same thing when they were babies. Oh, Lord, why did they have to die?

"You come with me an' help in the kitchen." Mavi reached out for Olive. "Mister Brooks, I keep the bedrooms clean. Y'all unpack while I fix up a hot meal."

Brooks showed Hattie a room at the back of the second floor. Mavi called it the sunset room because the evening sun cast its last light through the large open windows. "Why don't you and Olive stay in here?" He dropped Hattie's worn satchel on top of a walnut dresser, avoiding her glance in the mirror. "I've been thinking, Hattie. Maybe you should stay here awhile before we look for your aunt."

"Why's that?"

"There's something going on in town. That letter I got in Houma? It was from Sam, my old deputy, asking me to come here and help him. Now we're here, and Sam's not. It's not like him to just go off like that, not without telling Mavi and Jeb. There's got to be a reason for that. Sam doesn't do things without a purpose. I can't explain it; it's just a feeling I have. You and Olive should stay on here awhile. Maybe you could call it a former Sheriff's instinct."

He smiled at her in the mirror but thought to himself, *That way I can keep an eye on you two.*

"Well," Hattie dropped her satchel on a wide double bed, made up with a patchwork quilt in orange and yellow crazy strips. If she were suspicious, she didn't show it. She shrugged. "I guess it's fine. My aunt didn't rightly know when to expect me anyway."

Questions churned through his mind. *Was it just coincidence Hattie and Olive had shown up on his doorstep, needing an escort to Beaumont the same week Sam wrote to asking him to come?*

"That's fine, then. I'm sure Mavi could use your help. This is a busy time on the ranch. You can 'earn your keep,' as we say out here, for a few days. Let me talk to her and see if she can find you something to do. It would make me feel a little easier about leaving you with your aunt later on, once we know the town is safe. Especially since we never saw any sign of those men chasing you."

If Hattie realized he'd been poking for information, she didn't act like it. Instead, as he stared in the mirror, Hattie's green eyes fixed on him with an intent he couldn't fathom. "Your friend, Sam, maybe you ought to go out and look for him."

"Why?"

"Maybe something happened to him."

Now why would Hattie think that? What did she know? Brooks suddenly had a gut feeling Miss Hattie Munn knew much more than she would say. Unable to think of an answer, Brooks turned and left the room.

Hearing the sounds of a skillet clattering on the black iron range, Olive prattling, and the banging of a tin cup on a table, Brooks avoided the kitchen. He headed out the front door and around to the cabin behind the main house. It had been Sam's first home when he moved to Texas. Later, after Sam found and married a mail-order bride, he'd built the large *hacienda* for Irene and given the cabin to the Jacksons. Sadly, Irene was not made for life as a Western bride and soon left for parts unknown. Sam stayed in the big house, alone, except when he invited friends to come and stay a spell. Brooks and his family had been frequent guests.

Jed opened the cabin door and shouted, "Mister Brooks! Good to see you back!"

"Glad to see you again, too." They exchanged a few pleasantries about what had happened in the last six years and then Brooks grew serious. "Jed, Mavi says you haven't seen Sam in a few weeks. What do you know?"

Jed's brow furrowed and his dark eyes showed distress. Sticking his hands in the pockets of his worn overalls, he shuffled his booted feet in the dust before answering. "I don't rightly know if I know anythin', Mister Brooks. I guess you heard there's been talk around town 'bout the Avilas coming back in?"

Brooks nodded.

"Well sir, Mister Sam, he was right worried. He and Sheriff Storey went out a few times – tried to round up a posse to go with them, but most folks was too scared. Couldn't find a thing. Then this one night, me and Mavi heard a rider come up. Knock on Mister Sam's door."

"Did you see the rider? Know him?"

"No sir, but we heard him and Mister Sam talkin'. Mavi, she say maybe I should go see if everythin' all right. Before I could, Mister Sam came back here."

"What did he say? Was he concerned?'

A shake of the head. "No sir, he seemed fine. Said he needed to go out and talk to some folks in the mornin'. Told me and Mavi to keep things goin' around here. We had a man comin' out the next day to look at a horse Mister Sam planned to sell. He told me what to do about that. That's the last time I saw him."

"Mavi said you talked to people around town."

"Sure enough. Sometime Mister Sam stayed at the jail or the hotel if he didn't want the bother of ridin' back home. I waited until the end of last week and then Mavi said she had this bad feelin'. Wanted me to go ask.

"I talked to the Sheriff, and he was kinda concerned too. Said Sam never just took off like that without tellin' him before. He was right helpful. We talked to people at the mercantile store, both the saloons, that Father Kemp at the church. Nobody saw him. The next day we rode out to a few farms and ranches, but nobody seen him."

"Sam sent me this letter." Although it had been against the law to teach slaves to read a few years before the war, Jeb and Mavi had lived with a generous and benevolent master. The master's wife had taught all their slaves to read and write. When the War Between the States ended, they'd both been given their freedom.

"This looks like Mister Sam's handwritin'."

"I agree. But did he go off to confront Avila himself?"

"If he did, I'd be powerful scared, Mister Brooks. That Mateo Avila was bad – but from what I hear, his brother, Rafael, be a lot worse."

Brooks had a sinking feeling Jed was right.

"What d'you plan to do?"

"Tomorrow, I plan to ride around to a few of the nearby farms, see if anyone has seen Sam. Maybe you can send one of the neighbor boys to town with a note for Sheriff Storey to meet me out here. It might be best not to announce my arrival here just yet – especially if the Avila gang is nearby."

A peculiar sensation crawled up Brooks spine, the feeling his grandmother used to call "*someone walkin' across your grave.*"

Chapter Eleven

Hattie had just put Olive down for a morning nap when Brooks stopped her in the big front room. "Mavi and I had a long talk after breakfast. While you're here, you can help with the garden chores." He gave her a peculiar kind of smile that made Hattie feel uneasy. "Just until we find your aunt."

"You don't act like you believe I got an aunt," Hattie snapped, tired of pretending. "Like I made it all up." She pointed to the scratches on her cheek, scabbed over and healing. "Like I did this, an' tore my dress and stole – and everything."

Brooks backed away with a knowing smile, hands up to fend her off. *Sure is a cute little thing when she gets her dander up.* "Now, Hattie, I'm not acting any way at all. But you said yourself your aunt might not be expecting you yet. Since you're Sam's guest, I'm sure you won't mind helping Mavi. She usually hires a girl or two from town to help with the garden, but since you're here, you can help instead. You can earn your keep. I'll be back later."

Disgruntled, Hattie stalked into the kitchen where Mavi was putting away the breakfast dishes. "Brooks said I was to help you this morning. I got to *earn my keep.*"

Mavi laughed, which didn't make Hattie feel any less annoyed. "That Mister Brooks, he sure enough a funny one, all right! Well, grab a straw hat off a peg there and we'll head out to the garden before it gets too hot. Once that sun starts beating down, we'll be as wilted as a vine. I've been fixin' to put in some more tomatoes."

At Mavi's instruction, Hattie put on a straw hat and followed her to an open shed. Inside were long, flat tables that held small wooden boxes of plants. Hattie couldn't even begin to figure out which plant was what. Everything looked like green leaves to her. Hattie had seen gardens, of course; everyone grew their own vegetables and fruits – ordinary folks, that is. Mateo's gang had never stayed put long enough to plant a seed, much less wait to harvest anything. The only 'gardening' Hattie had ever done was to steal fresh produce as the gang ravaged someone's farm or pillaged a mercantile bin.

"Jeb plowed up a new spot of ground for us this morning. Bring some of the tomato plants," Mavi instructed, going to one table, picking up a stick and a roll of string. "I'll grab the hoe too. Let me stake us out a line, an' you can help me see if it's straight."

Hattie stood at the tables, uncertain which were tomato plants. The only tomato plants she knew were bulging with round red globes of tomatoes. She could remember times when Mateo, just to be mean, high stepped his fine stallion through a patch of ripe tomatoes. The horse's hooves trampled the plants, the fruit smooshing under the heavy steps, splatting the ground with bloody pulp. She'd never seen tomato plants just starting out. She grabbed up one of the flat boxes and hurried off behind Mavi.

"What you got there?" Mavi looked up from shoving a stake into the cool, freshly plowed dirt. "Why'd you bring the peppers?"

"Um, I ..." Hattie stared at the box in her hand. "I guess the sun got in my eyes."

Mavi shook her head, uttered a few mumbled words, and stalked off to the shed. When she came back, she carried two of the flat boxes with plants. "*These* are tomatoes." She set the boxes on the ground, then pressed one of the leaves gently between her fingers, bringing her hand to her nose. "You can always tell by the smell."

Hattie knelt, cautiously bending her nose to smell the tiny plants. Mavi watched her, a patient but speculative look in her eyes. The plants smelled earthy, almost spicy, and Hattie had to turn her head quickly as a sneeze overcame her.

Mavi smirked gently, then went back to her task of tying string to a stick, moving it down the long row of the plowed ground, as Hattie stood by and watched. "Is that straight?"

Uncertain what was expected of her, Hattie stared before answering in a timid voice, "I think so."

Mavi stalked back to where Hattie stood, checked the straight line of the row herself, then grabbed up the hoe. "I'll make us a furrow," she instructed. "You take a plant and cover it with dirt. Can you do that?"

Take a plant and cover it with dirt. It didn't sound too hard. Hattie pulled one of the tomato plants from the box, dropped it into the furrow and covered it with dirt. *That's not too hard. So, this is planting tomatoes.* The sun beat down on her head and sweat wet the back of her dress, but Hattie felt like maybe something might be going right for a change. *This must be how ordinary women spend their days.*

For the first time, Hattie began to wonder what it would be like to live on a ranch like this every day. *Could I live like this one day? With someone like ... Brooks?*

"No, no, no, girl!" Mavi yelped, running back down the row. "What you doin' there? You done covered up the whole plant!" Kneeling down, she dug out the plant Hattie had covered, set it upright with just the roots in the ground, and pushed a mound of dirt up under the green leaves. The small plant stood upright like a tiny green flag as she patted the brown dirt around it gently. "You got to put the *roots* in the ground, not the leaves. Ain't you ever grown anythin' before? You some fancy lady like master's wife?"

"Master?"

"Sure," Mavi said, "like on a plantation? Me and Jeb were slaves until Mister Lincoln freed us. We lived with Master Jedediah and his wife, Miz Jane. They owned us. We did all the hard work, like tendin' the garden and workin' the fields. Miz Jane never lifted a finger to do nothin' – not until after the war when all the slaves were gone." A small smile of satisfaction crossed Mavi's face. "I had to show her how to fry an egg. Imagine. A person so helpless they can't fry an egg!" She chuckled as if amused by the idea. "Had to show her how to find the eggs in the hen house first. That where you're from – a plantation?"

"No."

Mavi muttered to herself but went back to dropping in a few more tomato plants. "You finish this row and I'll bring out another flat. Can you do it like I showed you?"

This time, Hattie made sure to plant the tomatoes as Mavi had shown her. Apparently, they met with her approval. Going back and forth to the shed, they filled four rows with the small tomato plants.

"So?" Mavi asked as they both stopped to take a cool drink from the canteen Mavi had brought along. "Where you been all your life that you ain't never planted tomatoes?"

"Here and there," Hattie answered, uncomfortable with the questioning. She'd known when she agreed to follow *his* plan that there would be questions. But Mavi's questions made her look at her life in a new way, a squirmy way Hattie disliked.

"You rich folk?"

Hattie laughed and sputtered water from the canteen. *Rich, ha!* She'd seen plenty of rich folks in towns, others on stages as Mateo robbed their satchels, pulled glistening rings off their fingers, and yanked jeweled necklaces or tie clips off their fine satin and lace clothes. "Not hardly."

"Then where you been livin'?" Mavi persisted until Hattie felt pressured to answer.

"My Ma couldn't take care of me. She left me with some friends. I been living with them."

I lived with Mateo Avila and his gang. Sure enough not something she could blurt out to this knowing-eyed woman.

"Seems mighty strange a young girl like you never grew tomatoes," Mavi answered, placing the cap back on the canteen. "Time's a wastin'; let's get the rest of them rows planted."

The next few hours were hot, sweaty, and tiring as they planted six more flats of tomatoes. Hattie's face burned as the sun beat down, and her arms quivered from carrying loaded buckets of water to pour on the newly-planted tomatoes. She was used to hard work, but this was different. When Mavi declared them finished for the day, Hattie felt a rush of emotion as she looked at the field with all those brave little tomato plants waving in the sun. *I did something fine, something good. Those little plants will grow and make tomatoes to feed people like Mavi and Jeb. Maybe Brooks ...* Hattie had rarely felt such a feeling of powerful satisfaction as she did at that moment, standing in the muddy garden. *My hands helped do something, like a ... like a good person.*

"What'd you do for these," Mavi hesitated, "*friends* you lived with?" She gathered up the hoe and handed Hattie an empty bucket to carry.

"Cooked, washed, carried water, mended, whatever needed done, whatever they said to do."

Mavi's wise eyes stared at her, and she gave an odd chuckle. "Sounds like you was a slave too, jes' like me and Jeb. Even after President Lincoln freed the slaves, we was still pretty much stuck – nothin' to do, nowhere to go. The gov'ment promised, but didn't deliver. Wasn't 'til Jeb came out here to Texas and met Mister Sam that things went right for us. He pays us to work for him. We ain't slaves. We're free to go anywhere or do anythin' we want. Got our own home. A'course, if you like bein' with these people, that's a different thing there. Like how a woman does for a man, might seem like bein' a slave, but not when you get some satisfaction from being with him. When you do for love, it's different."

Love? Hattie wasn't sure she even understood what that was. No one in the gang loved her; her Ma had never loved her. When she thought of Mavi's words, it did make her out like a slave – like Mateo owned her.

What would it be like to be free like Mavi? To make her own choices, without someone else hollering orders and slapping her if she didn't move fast enough?

What would it be like to be an ordinary woman and have a home, to cook for a man – someone I loved? What would it be like to live on a ranch with someone like Brooks? The thought brought a blush to her face. Could something like that ever happen to her?

The questions pounded in her brain the rest of the afternoon. On her way from changing Olive into a fresh diaper and dress, she passed the bedroom where Brooks had dropped his saddle bags. Hattie stopped for a minute and sneaked a peek inside, darting a scared glance over her shoulder. *No one else is in the house.*

Heart racing against the bodice of her blue dress, Hattie crept inside. On top of a walnut dresser lay the shiny gold badge Brooks had shown her. There was also a piece of paper lying underneath. Curious, Hattie stared at the three names printed in pencil.

Francisco Avila. Edmundo Ramirez. Frank Stanton.

Hattie's breath caught in her throat. Even though she couldn't read many words, she knew how to read the gang's names. For a minute, she couldn't breathe. *Francisco!* The very person who had dropped her off near Brooks' house in Houma to follow Rafael's orders. Why had Brooks written them down?

Olive grabbed the badge, bumped Brooks saddle bag and it toppled to the floor. Everything spilled out in a jumble.

"Durn you, Olive," Hattie grumbled, frantic to right things before Brooks returned. "We're in here snooping and you're going to get us caught." She sat the baby down and picked up a couple of shirts, a pair of gray suspenders, mended socks and stuffed them back into the bags. A worn daguerreotype had fallen half under the dresser. Hattie stooped to pick it up, ready to stuff it out of sight when the little velvet case flopped open. With an intake of breath, she stared at the old, grainy image of Brooks, sitting in a chair, tall and proud. His face stared out sternly, looking almost fierce. A six-pointed star – his badge – gleamed from the chest of the dark suit he wore. The wide-brimmed hat he always wore rested across one knee.

Standing next to him, a delicate hand on his shoulder, was the prettiest woman Hattie had ever seen. She wore a white dress, all ruffled and lacy. The hand not on Brooks shoulder held a bouquet of flowers. She had a mass of hair piled on top of her head, with a few stray curls dropping down one cheek. Unlike Brooks, her face wore a sweet, gentle smile, and her eyes were shining like it was the happiest day in the world.

Who was this woman? Was she the woman who wore the dresses in the cedar chest – the very dress Hattie wore now?

"What happened to her?" Hattie whispered to Olive. The baby gurgled an answer, fussing when Hattie took the gold badge from her inquisitive fingers and placed it back on the dresser. "Why does Brooks have the gang's names written down? I've got to find out."

Hattie's stomach churned. She needed answers and she knew how to get them. *Tonight.*

Chapter Twelve

It was after dark when Brooks returned. Mavi had left a supper of beef and beans to warm on the black iron cook stove. Hattie hurried to set a plate before him. "Did you – did you find your friend?" Hattie asked.

Brooks shook his head dejectedly, his eyes sad. Hattie fought off the desire to throw her arms around his neck and hold him tight, like she would comfort Olive. *Like you care,* she berated herself. *He's gonna be dead soon.* For some reason a sick feeling boiled in Hattie's stomach. *He's a good man, an honest man. Why should he die?*

Earlier, while they cooked supper, Mavi had shared a little about Brooks. Although she didn't come right out and say, Hattie heard enough to know Brooks had been married, with two boys.

"Where are they now?"

"Dead," Mavi had whispered, "all dead." Then she clammed up and refused to answer any more questions.

"Thanks for supper," Brooks said after he pushed the food around his plate for a while. "I'm too tired to eat more. Goodnight."

"Goodnight."

After she'd washed up the supper dishes, Hattie climbed the stairs to her room, checked on Olive, and stood in her darkened room waiting for Brooks to settle in for the night. His restless wandering around the next room seemed to last forever. *Go to bed!*

Finally, the iron bed creaked; the oil lamp went out.

Once she dared, Hattie eased out of the dress and pulled on her worn pants, shirt, and boots. Waiting another lip-gnawing minute in the dark, she finally eased open the bedroom door and snuck out of the *hacienda*. She wished she dared saddle a horse from the corral, but Jeb might hear. Instead, she walked toward the back pasture, trying to remember the details of the secret meeting place.

Right before Francisco had set her on the path to Brooks' house in Houma, he'd given her directions on where to meet.

"We can't be sure when Shanton will head for Beaumont," Francisco had said, *"so I'll try to wait there every night until we can meet up. When you can, sneak away and meet me."*

"What if I can't get away?"

"You'll find a way, Chiquita," Francisco had assured her. *"It'll all work out. When this goes off like Rafael plans, I'm going to keep my promise to make him set you free. Maybe you can go off to a big city and find work."*

"Ha, doing what? All I know how to do is wash and clean up, steal, and rob. What kind of a job can I get with that?"

Hattie headed into the darkness, glad the moon lit part of her path. Off in the distance, a coyote howled, and another answered. From somewhere nearby, she heard the creak of the windmill and a gurgle of water. Francisco had scouted out Deputy Sam's ranch when Rafael first came up with his plan to get back at Brooks. He had told her to walk past the corral until she came to a small rise.

"There will be una cerca, *a fence, with a Texas longhorn,"* he'd advised. *"Make sure you keep clear of him! Walk about half a mile along the edge of the fence, and you will see a rocky outcrop. Go past that to a sycamore tree, and you will see a kind of shed where they keep branding tools."*

She stumbled a few times, her footing unsure on the bumpy ground. After her eyes adjusted to the light, she had no trouble following the directions or finding the shed.

"Hattie?"

A whisper out of the dark.

"Francisco?"

"You found me!" He came out of the gray shingled shed. "You got Shanton here. I knew you'd do it!"

Hattie denied it. "No, he came because his friend, the deputy, wrote a letter. Not because of me. He still thinks I'm lookin' for my aunt."

Francisco reached his arms around her to give her a hug. Like a big brother, he ruffled her hair and set it on edge. "It does not matter, he is here. Has he spoken about Sam, or the gang?"

"He's still trying to find Deputy Sam. He's not said anything except ..."

Francisco grabbed her shoulder tight and gave it a shake. "What do you know? Tell me!"

"Nothing! He just said there was trouble in town. Only, I saw a paper. It had names wrote on it. You and a couple of the others."

Francisco's eyes grew wide, and he stared off into the darkness. "You are sure? You never were much good at reading."

"I know how to read your name, and Frank's, and Edmundo. Why's he got your names on paper?" She began to let her suspicions out. "I know he wants to catch the gang.

Does he want you too? You were part of Mateo's gang before. What did you do to him?"

The gang had never kept her too much in their confidences. What little she knew came from overhearing whispered, often drunken, conversations as they sat around campfires. After Mateo had been hanged, the gang roamed around with Edmundo in charge. A year later, Rafael came from Mexico and took over. Even at fifteen, he was a natural-born leader, full of vengeance and ruthlessness. Until the past year, Hattie had never heard the hissed name of Shanton or knew how much they despised Brooks.

"He was family; of course I ride with him." Francisco answered. "I knew Shanton. Knew how vengeful he was toward all the Avilas. He was the reason Mateo and Sabine were captured. Hanged."

Francisco had always been friendly toward her. He never hit her or called her mean names, and treated her more like a little brother than a girl. Until tonight, Hattie had always trusted him. Now she wasn't so certain.

"What happened to Brooks' family? What do you know about that? That Mavi woman said they're all dead. Did you know that when you sent me here?"

Francisco's horse whinnied from beside the shed. At first, Hattie didn't think he planned to answer. "Yes, I knew he had a family." The words came out reluctantly.

"What happened to them?" The horrible truth hit her in the stomach like a punch. "Did you kill them?"

"Hattie, I cannot tell you right now. You don't need to know. All you need to do is follow Rafael's plan so he can get justice for Mateo, once and for all."

A sick feeling came to her stomach, like she might be sick right there. Francisco knew more than he was telling. Hattie hadn't seen all the gang's violent acts, but she'd witnessed too much horror not to have her suspicions.

"Why can't I know? You took me to Louisiana to get Brooks back to Beaumont. Made me steal a baby from an orphanage and pretend I had an aunt living here. You knew he'd come back. Now, you tell me why Rafael wanted him to come back here. Mateo killed his family, didn't he? That's why he got hanged. Not all those lies you all told me – that he was innocent. You tell me the truth!"

She had never spoken up to any of them, even Francisco, as she did then. Her hands clamped into fists and her face burned with rage.

"I cannot," Francisco's voice got low and intense. He caught her arm and held tight, hurting her. "My cousin is *loco*, but he's the boss. He says what happens. We do what he says. We have no choice."

"Why?"

"You know why? Because of Mateo!"

Hattie remembered hating Mateo as she had never hated anyone since. When he died, a week after her thirteenth birthday, she had felt an enormous relief, almost like his booted heel, pressing her to the ground, had been lifted off her chest. Then Rafael came from Mexico, seething with rage and ruthless violence, and pressed her right back into submission.

"You don't have to know more, Hattie. Just do your part. Watch Brooks, tell me where he goes and what he plans to do. Especially if he says any of the names on that list. Remember what I promised. If everything goes the way Rafael wants, then I will make him set you free. You can go anywhere; do anything you want. I'll make him give you enough money for a grub stake – set you up anywhere you want. But don't tangle with him, Hattie. Don't cheat him out of his revenge."

"I don't know. I gotta think this through."

"Here," he pulled a piece of parchment from his vest and pushed it into her hand, "two days from now, give this to Shanton. Tell him you found it in the deputy's house."

"What is it?"

"It's a map to where Rafael wants to exact justice. Two days."

Hattie ran back to the *hacienda* and stopped to get her breath by the corral. All seemed quiet. No lights shown from the cabin or the main house. On tiptoe, she snuck up to the wide front porch. Just before she stepped on the first step, she caught a sliver of movement at Brooks' window. Like a curtain had dropped. Holding her breath, she waited an agonizing second, but nothing happened.

I sure hope he didn't see me.

***

The next morning, Brooks stood on the porch of Sam's house, staring off into the distance. In front of him, Jeb was coming from the barn with a milk pail in hand, but Brooks could not stop wondering what Hattie had done last night. *Who did she go to meet? Am I suspicious for no reason? Maybe she just went for a walk. Sure, dressed in men's clothing, sneaking around. I thought she saw me at the window, but she came on in as if she didn't.*

What were you doing out there, Hattie?

95

"Mister Brooks," Mavi hurried up to the porch and handed him a letter. The wax seal on the back of the envelope had a pattern like one point of Sam's badge. Brooks recognized the bent corner of the left-hand star. "Young Ben Owens from the telegraph office came by a while ago. Said he rode out from town to give it to you." Mavi's hand shook as she handed it to him. She recognized the seal too.

"Thanks." Brooks opened the envelope to find a note. "It's not in Sam's handwriting," he told Mavi as his eyes glanced at the tight, ink spotted lines. "Although it's supposed to be from him." He read it out loud.

"Dear Brooks, Sorry I couldn't meet you when you got to the ranch. I'd have liked to welcome you in person. But I can explain it when I see you. I've been waylaid and I'm holed up. Remember that spot about seven miles from the ranch where we used to take your boys to swim? I will meet you there as soon as you get this. Sam."

Mavi kneaded her hands in her apron. The look of uncertainty on her face probably matched his own. "What you plan to do?"

"Ride out there."

"Alone?"

Brooks nodded. "Yes; if it's Avila's gang and they want me, I don't want anyone else getting hurt."

Mavi lloked like she wanted to say more but was wise enough to keep her fear to herself. "I'll be prayin' for you, Mister Brooks. An' prayin' you find Mister Sam ... alive."

He hurried up to his bedroom, took his gun belt from the dresser drawer, and strapped it around his waist. He pulled the Colt single-action army revolver out, spun the barrel to check it was loaded, and slid it into the holster hanging down his right hip.

Brooks sighed and strode down the rest of the stairs. Hattie came from the kitchen, her eyes riveted on the gun belt. "What's wrong? Where are you going?"

"None of your concern. Stay here with Mavi and Jeb. If ..."

"If what?" Her voice grew shrill. "Tell me where you're going!"

He shook his head as she followed him out the door. "There's something I must do."

"Don't go," she begged, green eyes pleading, "or take the Sheriff, or someone, with you."

"Stay here," he repeated, then turned and left her there.

Jeb saddled a horse and Brooks rode toward the place the note had mentioned. As the horse trotted forward, poignant memories flooded Brooks' mind. Picnics with Emily, Sam, and Isabel, before she left the ranch. His boys racing, gamboling like young colts through the tall grass.

As he neared the grassy meadow beside the quiet stream, Brooks kept a wary eye on his surroundings. There was a small hill off to the right where someone could hide easily enough. "Whoa," he whispered to the horse, reining him in. There was no one, just the eerie feeling of eyes watching.

Brooks pulled out his gun, kept it beside his right pant leg; no sense advertising its presence. "Sam?" he called. "Sam?"

A mockingbird flew up, startled, and spun off into the deep blue sky. "Anyone here?" His words echoed back to him before the world went still. Brooks caught sight of a mound near the stream.

A grave. A freshly dug grave.

Chapter Thirteen

His heart clenched and he knew. Even before he walked the horse over to the dirt mound, he knew. *Sam. Gone, too. Just like Emily and the boys.* A scream of rage bubbled up, but he pressed his lips tight to hold it in. He ached to shake his fist at the heavens, or shout vile imprecations, as he'd done the day he discovered his murdered family. Instead, he clenched his teeth and nudged the horse closer.

You deserved better than this, Sam. Better than a makeshift grave, a crude wooden cross stuck at the head of the mound. On top of the dirt, he recognized Sam's badge with the bent tip on one star's point. Years ago, during a bank robbery, a young bandit had shot Sam during his getaway. As Sam liked to tell the tale, punctuated by cheery guffaws and knee slapping, "Durned if that bullet didn't ricochet off my badge and hit that young varmint right in the leg. He screamed like a stuck pig." Even in his grief, the memory of Sam repeating the oft-told story curved Brooks' lips in a slight smile. *Oh, Sam.*

There was Sam's revolver, stuck into the mound, butt end in the earth. No question it was Sam's. He prided himself on keeping the mother of pearl inlay on the grip polished to a sheen. Scattered across the mound lay a worn leather vest and a slashed blue shirt, steeped in blood. The bloodstains on the shirt and the ragged rips showed Sam must have suffered a great deal before he died.

Brooks sat rigid in the saddle, eyes moist with tears. He focused on the crude cross, tied around with a colorful red bandana. He had seen such a bandana before. Mateo used to wear one to cover his face during sandstorms. It was meant as a message.

"I know you're out there," he shouted, turning from left to right in the saddle. "Whoever you are, show yourself! Come out and fight like a man! Just you and me. No defenseless women or children, no old deputy."

No one answered. Brooks felt eyes staring, gloating. His neck prickled with the eerie feeling that they were everywhere.

After an eternity, he turned and rode away, mourning Sam.

***

Sheriff's Office

Beaumont, Texas

"Sheriff," a long-legged boy said breathlessly as he ran into the jail, "you got a note here. Someone sent it in by my brother."

Sheriff Michael Storey, feet propped on his scratched oak desktop, reached for the note. "Thanks, Will. Maybe there's a word from Sam. I'm not sure where that deputy of mine has gotten too."

The letter wasn't from Sam but … He dropped his feet to the floor, mouth open in astonishment. Brooks Shanton – *The Golden Star*. The next part of the note caused a chill in his heart. *Sam dead!* Dependable, curmudgeonly Sam, dead and buried in a makeshift grave.

"Will, go get my horse from the livery. I need to ride out to Sam's."

Michael couldn't help his excitement as he rode along. *The Golden Star!* Brooks had been the reason he had yearned, even as a young boy, to become a Sheriff. He wanted to be as well-known, as full of justice as Brooks. It had been his dream since he'd been in short pants. Now he would get to meet him again and work with him. He'd been concerned about the Avila gang, their brutality. He and Sam had spent days riding with a posse to find they'd pillaged another ranch or killed another family, but he was no closer to catching them now than they'd been before. *Maybe Brooks will have some ideas.*

***

"Brooks Shanton!"

Brooks stared at the sheriff, reassured by the tall, broad-shouldered stature of the young man staring at him from the saddle of an American Quarter horse. "Michael, thanks for coming so quickly."

Brooks had come from Sam's grave, stopping along the way to send a neighbor's son into town with a note. As soon as he rode up to the ranch house, a spirit of unease settled on his shoulders. Sam would never dismount and tie his horse to the hitching rail again. Never take the porch steps two at a time with his wide-booted steps. Never snitch one of Mavi's warm pies from the kitchen windowsill.

I'm sorry, Sam. I should never have left you to fight this battle alone.

As he had come through the heavy wooden door, Brooks had stopped on the polished parquet floor of the entryway and glanced into the parlor. Sam had decorated the room for Isabel, his mail-order bride. The adobe walls were hung with Navajo rugs in bright reds and yellows. There were niches, one with a blue pottery jar and another holding a vase of bittersweet. The leather furniture was soft, comfortable, and worn to Sam's liking. It all made a pretty scene to surround Hattie and Olive.

Hattie had been sitting in a rocking chair, cradling Olive in her arms, humming to the baby. A shaft of sunlight came through the big picture window Sam had left curtainless. It beamed down on Hattie's blonde hair and touched an angel finger to Olive's twisted curls. They had looked so angelic sitting there.

Hattie showed up on my doorstep in Houma; she couldn't be a part of this. She's too young, too innocent. Too sweet and – stop that! Brooks tried to rein in his heart. *You aren't starting to care for this woman. You just feel sorry for her.*

I hope.

She looked so lovely rocking Olive, soothing her with gentle touches and caresses. *How does she fit into this with Sam? Does she know about the grave?* He couldn't put a finger on his uneasy feeling, but he felt like Hattie's appearance was no coincidence. He'd noticed Hattie's visible relief when she looked up to see him.

"You didn't find no trouble, then?" she'd asked, almost as if she feared the worst.

"Was I looking for trouble?"

"Well, I thought you was going out to look for your friend, the deputy."

It was then Michael rode into the yard and Brooks went out to meet him. "That's the Sheriff. Let me talk to him first."

"Brooks Shanton! I'm glad to see you back, but wish it was under better circumstances." Michael dismounted and came to shake Brooks' hand. His face shone with eagerness, like a little boy with a Christmas stocking. Michael had never denied that Brooks was his hero.

"Good to see you again, too."

"I was sorry to hear about Sam," Michael began, then choked up and took a moment to get his emotions under control. "Darn fool. He was bound and determined to try to track down Avila's gang on his own. I told him a dozen times not to be so foolhardy. You know, Sam. I was worried he'd try to head out without me."

"Tell me."

"Well, all I know is we got word from a ranch about thirty miles to the south that Avila's gang had hit a way station there. They took all the horses, supplies, killed the station master and his two young kids."

Brooks flinched, remembering two other dead children.

"We've been fighting this battle for years. Ever since you left. I figured after Mateo hung, things would quiet down, and they did for a bit. Then the rest of the gang made Mateo kind of a martyr to their cause and carried on. I've heard his brother, Rafael, came up from Mexico with a couple of other cousins."

"Francisco Avila? Is he still with him? Edmundo?"

"Far as I can tell. Anyway, they're like ghosts in the night. They've even hit the mercantile in town a few times, made off with enough supplies to keep them in food and clothing for a while. How they get in there, we never can tell. Me and Sam would ride out, try to follow their trail but it would just vanish. They must have a secret hideaway somewhere."

"I guess Sam got too close." Brooks thought of that freshly dug grave. He pulled Sam's letter from his shirt pocket and handed it to the Sheriff. "He sent me this letter, asking me to come to Beaumont."

Michael studied the letter. "Yeah, that's Sam's hen scratches."

Brooks saw Michael glance up at the window, turned and noticed Hattie looking out.

"You get married again, Brooks?"

"No," Brooks shook his head in denial, but his heart lurched with a small thrill of hope. *Hattie? A wife? My wife?* "That's Hattie Munn. I brought her out here to meet up with her aunt. I'd hoped to meet up with Sam first."

Sam.

"Let's ride out to this grave," Michael suggested, "see if we can find a trail. Maybe we can track down some of the gang this time – now that I have the Golden Star on my side."

"Don't expect too much, Michael. I've been a rancher for six years now; I'm not as sharp as I once was. I'm not sure I could even shoot straight."

Michael clapped a reassuring hand on his shoulder. "It'll come back to you. You didn't earn that nickname for no reason."

"Let me tell Hattie where I'm going." He went into the house and found Hattie pacing behind the front door. "I'm going out with the Sheriff to try and track down the people who killed Sam. You might as well know, he's dead. I found his grave this morning."

"Dead?" Hattie's face went a ghostly pale, and she reached out to steady herself against the stair railing. "He's … dead. You're certain."

"I found the grave and bloody …" He didn't say more but the look of horror on Hattie's face told him he didn't have to spell it out. "I'm going out to tell Mavi and Jed. Then Michael and I are going to see if we can pick up a trail. Stay here."

Hattie nodded and sat down on the bottom stairs as if her legs would no longer hold her up. "I'm sorry."

Brooks nodded acceptance of her consolation, but his thoughts churned.

What do you know about this?

Chapter Fourteen

Mavi came over to cook dinner, but her tears and grief were so overwhelming, Hattie sent her home. "I can fix me and Olive something."

The woman couldn't stop crying. "Mister Sam was so good to me and Jeb. Don't know what's going to happen to us now. He give us our little cabin and work, but what will happen to the ranch now? Why'd somebody want to go and kill him for? He was a good man. Why?"

Why?

"Me an' Jeb are goin' to ride over to some neighbors and tell them the news. You be all right here?"

Hattie nodded. *They won't hurt me.* Her lips twisted in a bitter sneer. *Not since I've done what they wanted.*

Why did they kill the Deputy? Hattie knew they hated Brooks; they blamed him for Mateo being hanged. She had never heard them talk much about the deputy, Sam. While she had never actually witnessed the gang kill another person, she'd overheard them talk and brag about how they'd done it. Maybe it was Francisco protecting her, or maybe Rafael didn't trust her not to tell if she were cornered. Even though she'd never actually seen it happen, a few times she'd been near enough to hear the screams, the gunshots, people pleading for their lives. Most of the time, she tried to close her mind off to it all, telling herself to be thankful it wasn't her.

What will happen to Brooks? What if the gang plans to wait until he's alone? Will they kill him?

Hattie put Olive down for a nap on the big walnut bed, looking around at all the pretty furniture in the bedroom. Brooks had told her how Sam picked out everything for his mail-order bride. The carved dresser and headboard, decorated with flowery curlicues and ivy. The tall, curved mirror with wooden feet. The orange and yellow crazy quilt and ruffled pillow shams. Hattie's stomach twisted at the waste. *Sam won't ever walk in this room again and remember his bride.*

The brutality and senselessness of it all badgered Hattie's mind as she pulled the door shut on the sleeping baby. How well her imagination could picture a bloody shirt, a grave. Her thoughts gave her no peace as she paced from room to room in the house of a man she'd never met. *I'm sorry, Sam. So sorry for my part in this.* A huge weight of guilt settled on her shoulders, and she couldn't stand still. *If they kill Brooks, his blood is on me.*

When the afternoon was well along, she heard a horse outside.

Brooks! He's safe!

Relieved, she hurried to open the heavy wooden door. Her heart dropped to the pit of her stomach. The rider was not Brooks. A tall lean man in a long brown dress dismounted and tied the reins of a sway backed horse to the hitching post. *A priest! Brooks is dead and he's come to tell me!*

Hattie grabbed the door frame and held so tight her knuckles turned white. Her heart skipped a beat as bile rose to her throat. *No, no, no!*

"Good afternoon." He lifted a funny shaped hat and gave her a courteous bow. "I'm Father Kemp, from Beaumont. Who might you be?"

"Hattie," she managed to whisper.

"I came to speak to Mavi and Jeb. Are they home? Sheriff Storey told me the sad news about Sam this morning. I came to offer my condolences and see if I can be of any assistance."

"I thought ..." She drew a deep breath, relieved he hadn't come to tell her about Brooks' death. *And why should you care? You aren't anything to him.*

But maybe this was a sign. Mateo had taught her a lot about signs.

"Come in, Padre." Hattie held the door open as the priest followed her inside. "Mavi and Jeb are real tore up about Deputy Sam. They went to tell some friends the terrible news. I guess they'll be back later."

"I'm sorry to hear that. I wanted to tell them that we all feel their loss. Tell me, my dear, were you related to Sam?"

"Who, me? Um, no ... I came out here to ..." Hattie figured she might not know a whole lot, but she'd heard enough superstitions from Mateo, Rafael, and the gang about what happened if you lied to a man of the cloth. You'd burn in hellfire forever. Hattie had never figured hellfire was any worse than the way she lived now, but she didn't particularly want to find out. Even as vicious as Rafael could be, he never hurt a priest or stole from a church. Rafael had deep superstitions about churches.

"I came out here ..." Hattie knew enough to know that priests were not allowed to tell secrets if you told them. "Can I tell you a secret? Will you listen and not tell anyone else?"

Father Kemp's eyes were deep blue, filled with compassion and wisdom. "If you wish, my child. What can I help you with?"

"Will I burn in hellfire for causing other people trouble?" At his confused look, Hattie explained. "I want to tell the truth. Even if – even if ..." *If Brooks hates me.*

"Speaking the truth is always a good beginning."

"But," Hattie tried to explain, wringing her hands together, "if I tell the truth, Brooks might get hurt worse. I don't want to hurt ..." *Him.* No, she couldn't tell the priest that.

"Brooks Shanton? He would be hurt by your truth?"

"Yes, sir. He brought me back here from Louisiana. I rode with this gang, and they had a plan. I was to go to Brooks' home and get him to bring me back here to Beaumont." Even spilling it all, Hattie kept the part about Olive to herself. Some instinct told her not to reveal the baby sleeping upstairs. *I don't want anyone to take her from me. Not even a priest. He'd send her back to the orphanage. I can't. I just can't.* The thought of handing her baby over to strangers ... *No, I won't!*

"Is this Avila's gang?" The priest asked. "You rode with them?"

Hattie nodded. Taking a deep breath, she continued her story. "Someone sent Brooks a letter his old deputy wrote. I think –" Hattie struggled not to cry. "I think that someone forced him to write the letter and tell Brooks to come here and I feel guilty because I knew they wanted me to make sure Brooks came." Hot tears of remorse dribbled from the corners of her eyes. "Honest, I didn't know Sam was gonna be dead, but if I had told Brooks the truth at the start, maybe he could have kept it from happening. And now I'm worried they plan to kill Brooks too. And I'm mad at myself for going along. All my life I've had to go along ..."

Hattie's words poured out to the compassionate listening ear. How her mother had sold her to the gang. The reasons

109

she'd had to cut her hair and dress like a boy. All the terrifying times she'd cried herself to sleep or been whipped and cursed like a piece of dirt. "Like a slave – like what happened to Mavi and Jeb before they were free. That's what I was and now I'm ashamed and I want to tell Brooks the truth, but it will hurt him and I ..." Realizing it was true, she spoke the thoughts out loud. "I don't want to hurt him. I think he's a fine man, honest and good. I don't want the gang to hurt him, to kill him."

After her blurted confession, the priest lifted a gentle hand. "There is a simple solution to some of this. While you can't undo what has happened before, you can tell Brooks the truth now. Warn him of the dangers to come."

"I can't!"

"You must," he advised, "If you let harm come to Brooks because you hide the truth, you will carry the weight on your shoulders for the rest of your life. His blood will be on your hands."

Hattie stared down at her white hands, imagining them stained with Brooks' blood.

No!

Chapter Fifteen

Sam's grave. Brooks shuddered at seeing it again. *Why, Sam?*

Michael dismounted, dropped to one knee, and placed a hand on top of the dirt mound. "Goodbye, old friend." He picked up Sam's revolver and badge, put them in his saddlebag. "I think he has a niece in Dallas. She might want to keep these."

"You reckon," he glanced up at Brooks, blue eyes damp with unshed tears, "we should leave him here?"

Brooks sat in the saddle, remembering happier days. Although they probably hadn't planned it, the gang had buried Sam in a favorite picnic spot. On many a summer day, Brooks and his family, Sam, Jeb and Mavi would settle down in the grove of cypress trees. Emily and Mavi would take off their shoes and stockings, roll their skirts to their knees and frolic in the water. George and James would splash and wade, giggle and pick up frogs. This was a good place – a happy place. "No, I think this is where he's meant to be. We had fine times here." He changed the subject, hardening his heart to the business at hand. "Let's see if we can pick up any sign of a trail."

They spent some time walking around the rocky outcropping after tying the horses to a tree nearby. Marks of footprints in the dirt showed where three riders had stood for a time. "Probably the ones watching you," Michael said. "After they left the grave for you to find."

They went back for the horses and began to follow the trail. They followed the footprints in the dusty ground for miles, but the trail eventually petered out. They led the horses in several different directions without finding any other clues.

"Guess that's all we're going to find for now," Michael said as the sun sank lower in the sky. "I should try to make it back to town before dark."

"Thanks Michael. I'll come in tomorrow – maybe we can get some men together and go looking. Whoever killed Sam shouldn't get away with it."

"I'm sure it was Avila's gang." Michael said. "That bandana, it's like they've left other places, flaunting their dirty work. Rafael is the dangerous one. The others, Francisco and Edmundo, pretty much do his bidding. Rumor says he's brought back a few other cousins from Mexico too."

"Who is this Rafael?

"Mateo's younger brother. A few years back, Sam caught wind of Rafael coming up from Mexico to avenge his brother's death. He hates you most of all and vowed revenge, but it's been six years; you'd think by now he'd either have killed you or given up."

As they rode along, Brooks told Michael the story about Hattie showing up at his door. Just as he thought, Michael reacted with surprise and suspicion. "You think someone sent her?"

"I don't know. She says she was on her way to meet an aunt in Beaumont. You ever heard of a 'Hattie Munn living anywhere in town? Or nearby? An older lady?"

Michael narrowed his eyes in thought, shook his head. "Not to my recollection, but she could live further out. A lot of new settlers have come in the past couple of years. Munn, Munn...that name does sound familiar." They rode a way before Michael suddenly heeled in his horse and stopped. "Munn! I knew that name rang a bell. There was a woman. You remember. When you were Sheriff. She lived down by the river in a shack and entertained a lot of men. Wasn't her name Munn?"

"Now that you mention it, I do. I kept thinking I recognized the name." Brooks felt those barbed wires of doubt poking at his memory. "Wasn't there some story about her having Mateo and his gang there sometimes? Didn't that come out in his trial?"

Michael appeared to give this some thought. "Maybe someone did mention it; like she could be a witness. But I think the district attorney decided not to use her. As I recall, she did anything for money to buy liquor."

"Sold her child?" Brooks interrupted, remembering a whole lot he'd forgotten. His Emily's rage at some bit of gossip she'd overheard at the General store.

"Brooks," she'd railed, stomping into his office. Her sweet face had been flustered, acting like a little banty hen protecting her chicks. *"Mrs. Ferguson heard from her washerwoman the most disgraceful story! That – that - woman down by the Little Ben River sold her child! You need to ride down and find out. A child! For money to get drunk on!"*

"I recollect that too. Didn't you ride out there one day?"

Brooks nodded, still uneasy about the encounter with a woman he knew as Belle. "Oh, she let me look all around the filthy cabin. No sign of a child. Said she had a little girl, but some relatives back East offered to take her in, give her schooling. I couldn't prove she hadn't. Had to assume my duty was done."

Or was it? If the rumors were true and Belle had sold her child to the likes of Mateo, was that ... Hattie? Just a baby abandoned to that barbarous villain?

Brooks' mind didn't want to wrestle around the idea. It felt too enormous to endure just then.

He left Michael at the crossroads to town and rode on to Sam's ranch. As he neared the house, he saw Hattie, pacing up and down on the wooden porch. Her first look as he came near enough to tie his horse to the hitching post showed relief. As he stared hard, guilt flushed her face. Like a fist to his gut, the truth hit him hard. The imaginings his mind hadn't wanted to believe.

"You knew!" They weren't the first words he planned to shout, but suddenly it all came broiling out. Sam's grave, the memories of finding Emily and his boys shot and left to die. Murdered by Mateo's gang. "You knew Sam was dead! Somehow you were sent to lure me back here. In case Sam's letter wasn't enough!"

"No, I ..." he could tell by her sharp intake of breath and the sudden flush to her cheeks that he'd hit the truth. His barbed wires of doubt had stood him in good stead once again. Why, then, did he feel sick to his stomach and disillusioned with life? *I think I felt like I could ... love her.*

"Tell me the truth! You were sent to lure me back here, weren't you?"

A timid nod.

He dredged up his memories of all the half-remembered gossip about Belle and her friendliness with Mateo, the little girl who was there and then gone. Some of the women from town, upset because Belle suddenly had money for a whole keg of whiskey. Enough to get her sufficiently boozed up to drown in the river one night. He had pulled her damp, limp body from the water himself, her yellow hair floating like seaweed around her bony shoulders and shabby dress.

"You were part of them, Mateo's gang."

To his horror, Hattie didn't deny a thing. "You have to understand how it was for me ..."

"You killed my family!" he interrupted, clenching his fists to keep from grabbing Hattie and shaking her hard. He was only too aware of how dangerous it could be to let his rage out, but he couldn't help himself. "Emily and my boys! You helped murder my family!"

This set her on fire, and she clasped her hands together, almost as if in prayer. Facing him, she pulled herself up to her full height. "I didn't even know you had a family! And when Mateo went on his first rampage, I was only thirteen years old! My mother sold me to him when I was six! Just a baby! I ain't never killed anybody!"

"You're a liar. If you rode with them, stole with them, you've killed with them."

"No, I did not." Each word came out as snappy as a whip's lash.

"Then why are you here? Why did you show up at my door?"

"Because they promised me if I got you here, I could go free. I could live my own life. They were gonna give me money to get started somewhere else."

"You lured me here for money!" He sneered. "You knew they'd killed Sam."

Olive cried out from the bedroom, woken by their shouting no doubt. Hattie didn't go to her right away, talking, trying to convince him of the impossible. Her small hand grabbed his arm, held tight even when he tried to shake her away.

"I didn't know any such thing! Sure, I heard them talking, but I didn't know who they were talking about. I never met your deputy. Didn't even know much about you except what they told me. They didn't tell me all their plans."

"You are a liar!" he shouted again, but not as forcefully. Hattie's look spoke of sincerity, not lies. Those green eyes stared into his own and never blinked or faltered. Maybe Hattie was as much a victim in this whole tragedy as Emily and his boys. Mateo had used her to his own ends and now Rafael was doing the same. He wanted to hate her; to fuel his anger and take out the rage on her.

I can't.

Brooks took a steady breath.

Olive screamed louder.

"Go get the baby," he said, turning with a sudden need to put some distance between them. "I've got to stable my horse."

Chapter Sixteen

Frustrated, Hattie climbed the stairs like an old woman, each step a mountain. Tears of rage filled her eyes as she went to pick up Olive. The baby had wet herself, so she spent a few minutes changing the linen diaper, soothing her, brushing those sweet curls away from her sleep-flushed face. The baby, sensing Hattie's mood, or maybe upset by the tears splashing down on her little face, continued to fuss and squirm.

"It's all right, baby, it's all right," Hattie crooned. She sat on the side of the bed and let Olive settle back down. As Hattie patted her back, the baby closed her eyes and tucked a thumb in her mouth. It wasn't long until she'd nodded back to sleep. Hattie kissed the rosy cheeks and tucked her back into the crib Mavi had borrowed.

I'm not giving you up. No matter what anyone says.

Once the baby looked asleep for the night, Hattie turned the lamp down low and eased out of the room. She went down the stairs, hoping Brooks had calmed down. To her relief, he seemed to have cooled off a bit as he stabled his horse and was now in the kitchen. He poured a cup of coffee as she walked into the kitchen and motioned her to sit across from him at the table.

His first words gave her courage. "I'm sorry, Hattie. I realize you weren't personally responsible for the deaths of my family. Like you said, you were just a child. But I don't understand how you could stay with them later, when you knew what they were like."

Hattie sat down, shrugged. "Wasn't any choice. I don't remember much about my Ma. There *was* another lady sometimes. I'm not sure who she was, but she taught me how to sew and to cook a few things. Ma ..."

"Your mother drank and entertained men," he stated bluntly. Hattie didn't need an explanation. She'd seen enough of the gang doing the same thing, sometimes using *her* as the entertainment, much to her shame. "She sold you like a piece of livestock. Just for money to buy liquor."

It hurt having him say it right out like that, but Hattie couldn't deny any part of it.

"One day Ma told me I had to go with Mateo. Wasn't until a few years later I knew she sold me to him and his gang." Even though she tried to talk in a matter-of-fact voice, Hattie couldn't help the trembling of the words. "I had to do what they said, or I'd get whipped. Some days I'd be so sore from being whipped I could hardly walk."

Brooks winced and grimaced down at his coffee. His knuckles clutched the mug until they turned white, like if he let loose of the mug he might punch something.

Hattie took courage from the expression and hurried on, remembering what Father Kemp had said. "Oh, I guess they were glad enough to have me cook and wash up, fetch, and carry. I was small, too. Guess Sheriff Storey told you how the mercantile got robbed and no one knew how. They used to put me through a window. I'd unlock the door and we'd take what we needed, lock it back up after we stole. Mateo, he thought that was right clever. But I never *ever* killed anybody. Ever. I hated when they did ..."

She remembered the woman who owned the teapot. Shuddered. "It made me sick."

"Wasn't there ever a time you could get away? Tell a Sheriff or someone. Ask for help. There had to be people who would take you in."

Hattie shook her head. "You don't know what it was like. Every day I just wanted to live until the next. Francisco, Mateo's cousin, he said their life wasn't right for a girl. He got them to promise if I led you back here to Beaumont, then I could leave and go free. Francisco's always treated me good."

"What would you do when you go free? Where would you go?"

"I'm not rightly sure. Being here, talking to Mavi, I kind of see how good it might be to live my own life and not be afraid all the time." Hattie plucked at the skirt of the blue dress, not wanting to look into Brooks' eyes. Afraid he might be condemning her – or worse, pitying her. "Only, I'm not sure Rafael plans to keep his promise. He's good at going back on his word."

"I'd like to believe you Hattie," Brooks said, taking a drink of coffee, "but you've lied to me from the second you showed up at my door. You conspired with the Avilas to lure me here. You knew my deputy was dead."

"No! I didn't know that." *He has to believe.* "I knew they made him write a letter asking you to come, but I didn't know what else they planned."

He shook his head sadly, as if he might not believe her. Hattie wondered if she believed it herself.

They sat in silence while the sounds and scents of life outside sifted through the windows. A piglet squealed in protest. Another piglet snuffled and snorted. The windmill creaked out a rhythm as it pumped lifegiving water into the trough. The barnyard smells wafted in, followed by the warm, comforting scent of sun-bleached linen drying on the porch rails.

"When I went to your house in Houma," Hattie tried to explain, like the priest had suggested, "I just wanted to do a

119

good job and make Rafael keep his promise to let me loose. That was my only plan. But then, you were different than the men in the gang. You were honest, I could tell that right off, and kind. Nobody ever cared about me before like that – whether I had clean sheets on a bed or even if I had a bed. And I don't know if you can believe me or not, but once I knew how you were, I didn't want to go through with it. I didn't know how to stop you from coming back here. I didn't have any money to go anywhere else and I had Olive."

Please don't ask me about her.

"Were you attacked on that stagecoach?"

"Wasn't ever on a stagecoach," she said, not meeting his eyes, those honest blue eyes. "Francisco dropped me and Olive off. Said to keep walking until we got to your cabin. He said you were the kind of man who wouldn't let a lady be stranded. They thought even if you didn't believe Sam's letter, you'd bring me back to Beaumont."

Silence.

Hattie tried again, desperate to have him trust her. "Honest, once I knew how you were, I didn't want you to get hurt. I wanted to tell the truth."

He shook his head. "I find that hard to believe, Hattie. I'm not sure I can trust you."

"It's true." Hattie reached for a way to make him believe. Maybe Father Kemp's offer to pray for her was working already. The perfect solution popped into her mind. "I can take you to them. I know where they'll be! Francisco told me the other night when…"

"I saw you sneak out."

120

Hattie flushed at spilling the secret but forged ahead. "I'm supposed to take you to a place in two days. Francisco gave me a map. It's so Rafael can ..." *How did he say it?* "He wants to 'exact justice.' Whatever that means?"

"Exact justice? Where is this place?"

"I can give you the map." Hattie sat up straighter on the wooden chair. A tremor of terror shot through her body. *You're going against them. They won't like that.* "But you got to protect me. Once they find out I've told, they won't let me live."

Brooks didn't appear too eager to take her up on the offer. "I don't know. Why should I trust you now? You've lied and led me on for the last few days."

"I guess you can't know for sure. But what else are you going to do? I'm the only one who knows where they are. I can give you the map. You'll have the jump on them. They won't know I told you."

Believe me, Brooks. Please.

She saw in his eyes the moment he agreed. His was a steely-eyed, determined gaze. He would trust her and not back down. "All right. Sam would have done the same for me. I'll bring his killers to justice."

Chapter Seventeen

The next morning found Brooks in Beaumont, startling Michael out of his breakfast biscuits with the news of what Hattie had shared.

"Are you sure you can believe her?" Michael asked the same question Brooks had wrestled with though a long, sleepless night.

"I guess so – it's all we've got to go on. Can you get a posse together? It's a few hours' ride outside of town. Hattie gave me a map."

"A posse? Well," Michael hesitated, "that's going to be hard to come by. Most of the town is too terrified of the gang to do more than hope they don't come near them. The last time we tried to track them down, we lost two good men when they got ambushed. We'd split up. Tom and Dave rode into a gulley following a trail. A few hours later, we found their bodies, slumped over their horses, and decided to head back into town. Since then, no one dares help me. I can recruit a couple of the boys as temporary deputies to keep watch here in town, but if we ride out, it's just you and me."

Brooks didn't like the odds, but what choice did he have? "How soon can we leave?"

It wasn't long until they were on the trail, following the crude map Francisco had given Hattie. Thankfully, as they had ridden out of town, two temporary deputies had offered to join in the search. Both were experienced lawmen, so they knew how to approach Avila's gang without sounding an alarm. By mutual consent, the four men rode single-file for the first hour, silent and vigilant. After a short break to water the horses, they spread out in a line and kept as far from one another as possible. Any lookout for the gang would notice only a single rider at a time, not a posse bent on justice.

They'd been riding for a few hours when they came upon a rocky ridge that overlooked a valley. Smoke curled into the blue sky from a fire down below. Horses whinnied and the muted voices of men echoed upward. *The gang?* A mixture of tangy manure and woodsmoke tickled the nose, signaling an encampment.

Brooks and Michael had come together at a fork in the path about a mile back. The other deputies had ridden past, then circled back to surround the valley. No one had seen a lookout. Using hand signals, Brooks gestured to Michael to lead the horses back down the trail and tie them to a tree. He then motioned the deputies to circle around and come in from another angle.

Pulling out his Colt revolver, Brooks crawled along the edge of the ridge, careful not to dislodge any rocks or give himself away. Close to the edge, he peered over at the camp. It comprised a couple of gray army tents, a crude corral of fresh-cut logs, and a campfire with an iron kettle hanging above it. Three or four men stood around the campfire; another sat on a log pulled up beside it and poked something in a cast-iron skillet.

Francisco Avila. Brooks would remember that face forever – he had clashed with him before. Hattie said Francisco was 'nice' to her. That, he couldn't fathom. The man was as ruthless as Mateo in many ways.

A dark-haired man dressed in blue trousers and a colorful red shirt seemed to be the leader. A wide Mexican sombrero hung down his back. As he turned to point to one of the horses, Brooks caught his breath. If he hadn't watched the life drain from Mateo's body at the end of that rope, he would have sworn the man was him. The olive-skinned face, a swatch of black mustache, the way he used his long, slim hands as he gestured to the other men; the resemblance was uncanny. He wasn't close enough to see if the man's brown eyes burned with the same evil glint. A shudder went through Brooks' body.

"Who is that?" he whispered when Michael crawled up beside him. "In the sombrero?"

"I'm not sure," Michael answered. "It could be Rafael, Mateo's younger brother. I've never actually seen him."

As they watched, the man who resembled Mateo mounted and rode off toward the west with four other gang members, leaving one lone man behind. *Francisco.* They lay hidden for a few minutes, deciding on a plan of action.

Michael whispered, "What should we do? Wait for the others to come back or take that man now?"

A blood lust, a wave of rage, filled Brooks' heart. "No! I want to take him, now! That's Francisco Avila." He pulled the golden badge from his shirt pocket and took a minute to pin it to his brown leather vest. "I'm still a lawman, and I've wanted to capture that man for years."

"You're the Golden Star," Michael said. He clamped a hand on Brooks shoulder. "You know best; if you think you need to do this, go now. It's your fight." Michael pulled his own Colt from a holster and pointed it down toward Francisco. "I'll cover you."

Easing down from the ridge, Brooks untied his horse, grabbed up the reins and chose a cautious path down into the valley. As he rode closer, aware of Michael somewhere behind him, he kept himself hidden as much as possible. Any shower of loose rocks or slight movement might cause Avila to go for his gun. As Brooks remembered, he favored a Sharps Rifle. It was a single-shot, full-bore rifle chambering powerful 50-70 ammunition. Francisco had an accurate aim and rarely missed. If he chose to fire on Brooks, a single shot might guarantee his death.

Brooks hoped to catch Francisco without the rifle – unaware and unarmed. The chance came easier than Brooks dared hope. Whistling, Francisco grabbed a bucket, left the rifle leaning against the tent pole and went to the creek for water.

Now!

Brooks charged across the grassy clearing to the edge of the creek. The horse under him galloped full force at Brooks' urging. Caught off guard, Francisco uttered a curse, threw the bucket, and ran toward the rifle. Brooks intercepted him, riding the horse between Francisco and the tent. The horse pawed the ground with impatience, the large hooves coming dangerously near Francisco's venomous face.

"You!" Francisco spat the word out. His eyes darted furiously to the rifle just out of reach. "What are you doing here?"

"I came to get you and those cowards you call a gang."

"Cowards we are not!"

Brooks stared with revulsion at the man's sun-browned face, creased with care and wrinkles, the greasy hair he shoved off his forehead. Francisco's brown eyes glared back in hatred.

"You killed my family."

Francisco snarled, denied. "I did not! It was Mateo who killed your family. But justice was done, was it not? You killed my cousin – the sole support of his family. A life for a life – is not that what your good book says. Is that not how justice is given by your law?"

"Justice?"

Brooks growled the word, jumped from the saddle, and went for the man's throat. Rage, such as he'd known only on the day when he found Emily and the boys' brutalized bodies, made him see red. His hands went around the man's throat, and he squeezed tight … tighter … willing to squeeze the breath out of the man he hated.

Francisco surprised him by kicking his knee, knocking Brooks off balance. Brooks went down on his hands and knees, rolled over, and tried to stand upright again. Francisco countered with a vicious kick to his gut. Startled and breathless, Brooks gasped, gulping for air as Francisco began to crawl swiftly toward the rifle beside the tent.

Brooks pulled his Colt and aimed at the man's head, intent on killing him. In the distance, he heard horses galloping toward them. Hoping, in the split second of thought, that it was Michael or the deputies and not the rest of the gang. Instead, he heard Hattie scream, "Stop! Stop, don't kill him!"

By that time Francisco had scrambled close enough to grab the rifle, to jerk it back and cock the lever. Brooks aimed. Francisco rolled left and the bullet hit his leg. Francisco screamed and dropped back to the ground, blood spurting through his fingers as he tried to staunch the wound. Brooks stood and walked to Francisco. He stood over the man, gun drawn, ready to pump the five remaining bullets into his worthless body. To erase one name from his list of revenge.

Before he could pull the trigger, Hattie galloped up, jumped off the horse and threw herself against his chest, blocking him from Francisco. "No, don't! Don't kill him, please!"

On the ground, Francisco, writing in pain, cursed, and glared at Brooks.

"Get out of the way, Hattie."

"NO!"

She stood her ground, blocking him as Michael and the other deputies rode up. "Brooks?" Michael asked, "What do you want us to do?"

"We can string him up right here," Jake, one of the deputies, said. "Nobody can say it wasn't justified. Not after what he did to your family six years ago. Or to Sam."

"I had no part in that!" Francisco squirmed, blood spurting through his fingers. "Their deaths are not on my hands. I am not such a coward I kill little boys. Or women."

"He's telling the truth," Hattie screamed, kneeling beside Francisco. "It wasn't him. It was Mateo and Edmundo."

"Brooks?" Michael asked again, giving him the choice, either to hang Francisco there or to shoot him. "It's up to you. We won't say a word. The law will justify it."

The other deputies muttered among themselves, one pulled out a length of rope already tied into a noose.

"The Golden Star," Hattie sneered, bringing Brooks back to reality. Tears spilled from her green eyes and streaked paths down her dusty cheeks. She punched his chest hard with her two small fists. "You ain't no different than them. You hate just as bad. You kill and say it's *justice.*"

As fast as he'd raged, he cooled off and stared down at his golden badge. *Hattie's right. Lord, forgive me, she's right. I do hate as bad as Mateo and Francisco.* Suddenly ashamed, he glanced around at the other men's faces. Did a man so consumed with hatred deserve to wear a badge? To take the law into his own hands? A reputation, he realized, could become as tarnished as the golden badge he wore. His shame came as quickly as his hatred for Francisco had taken over.

"No." The words were painful to say, but he knew they were right – even when Jake sneered and gave him a scorching look, branding him as a coward. "We'll let the law decide."

"Okay," Michael agreed, "let's take him into town and put him in jail. We'll have doc fix him up before we question him."

"Michael, I'd rather we take him back to the ranch and question him there." Brooks could see the deputies' disdain for this idea. He wondered if Francisco might have an 'accident' if it was left to them to ferry the bandito to Beaumont. "We don't want innocent people hurt if the gang raids the town searching for him. If no one knows we have him, the town will be safer."

"No one will be safe when Rafael finds out," Francisco spewed out as they loaded him on a makeshift litter. "You will all die."

Chapter Eighteen

Rafael Avila watched the whole scene from a hollowed-out rock where he'd hidden after hearing the gunfire. He'd sent his other men on a short scouting mission to see what might be happening on Sam Rathbone's ranch. It was too late to call them back when he caught sight of the Sheriff and several other men approaching their camp. The sun glinted off the gold badge on a tall, broad-shouldered man. *The Golden Star! Then the man must be Brooks Shanton. Francisco said Hattie had lured him to the ranch, just like I hoped.*

What are you doing, Brooks Shanton?

He could have warned Francisco the men were watching him, but he didn't. There was something about Francisco he didn't like – even if the man was a cousin. *"A distant cousin,"* Mateo had often sneered. *"A cousin whose loyalty is questioned."* No, Rafael did not like Francisco, because he was soft. Always the whining to stop the killing, the violence, to go back to Mexico. Always taking up for Hattie, who was nothing more than chattel.

Hattie! Rafael had no illusions about Hattie. To Mateo she had been a servant, a plaything. His brother had told him on a rare visit to Mexico how he bought the girl from her mother for the price of several bottles of whiskey. Later, the woman, regretting her decision, wanted the girl returned.

"But," Mateo's dark eyes had glistened with macabre delight, *"one night Belle took a little tumble into the river. Goodbye, Belle."*

As he watched the scene unfold in the valley, Rafael ground his teeth, enraged that he could not confront the men below. He longed to slice their hearts out with his sharpened Bowie knife, to rip their livers out and feed them to the coyotes. He saw through a red haze as he watched the men ride away, taking Francisco and Hattie with them.

When it felt safe to leave the hideaway, Rafael seethed as he rode toward the gang's secondary hideout – a precaution Mateo had perfected years earlier. Everyone in the gang knew if one campsite were compromised, they could rendezvous at the second hideout.

"Hattie Munn, you are a dead woman," he fumed. "You are a *renegada*, a turncoat. And you, Francisco. You will pay, my friend. You will pay."

Even though one of the men had wounded Francisco, Rafael saw no reason for his comrade to go willingly. *If it were me,* Rafael thought, *they would not bind me to a litter and carry me away. I would curse and tear them apart with my teeth. I would rip their hearts out with my bare hands.*

As he neared the hideout, he heard the unmistakable sound of a weapon being cocked. "It is me," he announced to Edmundo, who stood guard.

"What happened?" Edmundo lowered his Sharps rifle and reached out to grab the reins as Rafael dismounted. "Where are the others?"

"They will return. I sent them to scout around the Deputy's *rancho*." He stomped over to the campfire, sat on a log, and reached for the tin coffee pot. "Francisco is captured."

"No!" Edmundo dropped down beside him. "How?"

Rafael poured a tin cup of coffee and held it between his browned hands. Barely able to speak the words through tight-lipped anger, he related how he had watched the Sheriff and the legendary Brooks Shanton capture Francisco.

"Then your plan worked," Edmundo's face twisted in a grim smile of satisfaction. "You got the Golden Star to return, to come out of hiding. Now, we will hang him, as he killed Mateo and Sabine."

"Yes," Rafael agreed, staring into the orange and golden flames of the fire. "We will kill Brooks Shanton and the sheriff, and anyone else who assisted them in this injustice. You must know, my *muchacho*, Francisco and Hattie are turncoats. They played right into the Sheriff's hands. They are now the enemy. They, too, will die."

Edmundo knew better than to question Rafael's plan. Knowing it was best to stay clear of the leader when his eyes grew dark and his face twisted in remembrance, Edmundo busied himself with grooming the horses and starting a pot of rabbit stew for supper. After a while, the other members of the gang came riding back, learned of Francisco's capture, and sat around in uneasy camaraderie. They ate the stew and waited for Rafael to tell them what to do next.

Frank, who had ridden with Mateo, questioned as night fell, "What are we gonna do?"

"We will kill them! Just as Brooks Shanton killed my brother Mateo." Rafael's rage had grown stronger in the hours since Francisco's capture. "We will avenge Mateo's death."

Rafael jumped from the log where he'd been sitting. Rage seized his heart. He took out his anger with a sharp kick to the fire, upsetting the coffeepot and a cast iron skillet of bacon. The coffee spewed into the flames and hissed as Rafael snatched up the tin coffeepot and threw it into some brush. Frank scrambled to escape his wrath.

No one dared question him. Rafael gazed into the fire, the flickering flames reflected across his face. He heaved a sigh that came from the very depths of his soul. In a quiet, softer voice he began to speak. "My brother, Mateo, he was a good man. He took care of his family." The other members of the gang had heard the story many times, but knew better than to interrupt Rafael when he got into this mood. "He sends money home to me, my mother, my *abuela*. We lived well. We had enough."

Frank muttered an agreement. "Mateo lived for his family. All he did was for them."

Rafael nodded. "One day, no money. No money for flour to bake bread. No money to pay the doctor when *abuela* grows too sick. We grow hungrier and hungrier. I must go out and steal …" he spoke the word as if it left a terrible taste in his mouth. "I, Rafael Avila, must take so we may eat."

One of the men shifted in his seat, jangling his spurred boots.

"I had to learn to be a man quickly, to steal – even though I knew this to be wrong. At such a young age, I had to go with another gang to learn their tricks, to learn to steal and maim, to kill. I had to harden my heart to the screams and the begging, *'Oh, let me live.'* Why? Why should others live when my family did not? So I vowed that one day I would kill this man who took away from my family, who led us into this life of evil."

Someone coughed and poked the fire. Flames and a shower of cinders shot into the darkened sky. A troubled silence surrounded the men as they waited for Rafael to continue.

"*Abuela* dies. I am left to wonder. Where is Mateo? Why do we not hear? And then the news comes. Mateo and Sabine are hanged. Murdered by this sheriff known as the *Golden Star*."

Edmundo repeated Brooks' title like a curse and spit into the fire.

"Didn't Mateo promise the sheriff there would be trouble if he didn't stop hounding them?" Jefferson, one of the newer gang members asked. He had never ridden with the legendary Mateo but agreed wholeheartedly with anything Rafael proposed.

Rafael nodded, gazing sorrowfully into the fire. "I read in the newspapers; this Golden Star says at the trial Mateo killed his family. Was this true? If it was true, it was not murder as this Brooks says. It was not murder, but *justice*. Mateo's justice. If this Brooks Shanton had left Mateo alone so he could feed his family, nothing would have happened. Mateo promised revenge. Brooks had his warning. If he had listened, his family would not have died."

A few mumbles of agreement came from the circle of men.

"He should have listened."

"Left Mateo alone."

"Viva Mateo!"

Rafael stood and stared hard at each man seated around the campfire. "I vowed when I came from Mexico, I would have my revenge. I would avenge my brother's death. I vowed I would not stop until all those responsible also die, especially Brooks Shanton.

"He will pay for my *abuela* dying and my family without food. My little sisters' stomachs shriveling in because we had no money to buy flour to make bread. Mama had to leave my sisters on the church steps. It broke her heart, and she, too, died."

"We're with you, Rafael," Edmundo declared as he stood to clasp Rafael on the shoulder of his black vest. "We once pledged our allegiance to Mateo. Me, Frank, Sabine – but now we have joined you. Mateo was once our noble leader. We pledged to follow him. Now, we pledge the same to you, my friend. You, Rafael Avila, are our leader now."

"*Si!*" Came the shouts as the other men stood to clasp Rafael on the back or shoulder. "Rafael is our leader, and we will follow him. He is our Mateo!"

In the light from the dying fire, Rafael's face took on an eerie glow. "We will avenge Mateo and Sabine. I make a declaration! Anyone who helps the Golden Star will die. Hattie and Francisco are now the enemy too. They must all die!"

"Die! Die! Die!" The sinister portents screamed into the blackness of the night sky.

Chapter Nineteen

Early the next morning, Brooks and Jeb had just finished grooming the horses and letting them out to pasture when Michael Storey rode into the farmyard.

"How were things in town last night?" Brooks asked.

"Quiet. I thought I'd come out and take Francisco into custody and put him in jail. I've already sent a telegraph to the US Marshall from Houston to come get him. The sooner he's off our hands, the safer I'll feel. Has he said anything about where the rest of the gang are hiding?"

"Come on in the house," Books suggested. "I've got him locked up in the bedroom off the kitchen. He's handcuffed to the iron bedpost and not going anywhere with that injured leg. Mavi tended to him last night – got the bullet out – but he's unconscious now and in rough shape. The wound is inflamed, and I'm not sure he could manage to ride two miles, much less twenty, into town. I think it's infected. He needs rest and quiet. Why don't you let him stay here? That way if the rest of the gang comes looking for him, they won't shoot up the jail or the town."

Michael took off his Stetson as he came into the parlor of the ranch house. "I guess that would ease tensions in town. A lot of folks are barricaded in their houses, afraid the gang will come in and get revenge. One of those loose-lipped deputies spread the word we'd caught Francisco. Now everyone expects Rafael to terrorize the town."

"All the more reason to keep him here," Brooks urged. "He's not going anywhere with that busted leg."

"I guess if you keep him here, I can let word get around that he's not in town ... but I don't like to leave you out here like a sitting duck with the women and baby. What will you do if the gang finds out he's here?"

"Me and Jeb are here," Brooks reassured him, "and Mavi can handle a rifle if she has to. Come into the kitchen and have some pie and a cup of coffee. Mavi baked one of her famous apple pies this morning."

"That sounds fine. I've got something else I wanted to talk about anyway."

In the kitchen, Olive sat on a wooden chair, a towel tied around her waist to keep her in place. Hattie sat next to the baby, spooning bites of egg and mush into her pursed mouth.

"She's looking right pretty today."

As if she knew they were talking about her, Olive gurgled and gave the Sheriff a wide, eggy smile. She waved a silver spoon in one hand and reached out to tap the table, playing a baby game of her own.

Hattie grinned as she swiped a rag across Olive's messy mouth. "About the prettiest baby I ever saw."

Brooks poured a cup of coffee and cut a piece of apple pie. He sat the food before Michael but noticed the man's fidgety impatience. *Something else is wrong.* "What was it you wanted to talk about?"

Michael shifted in the seat, picked up the fork, poked at the pie and dropped it on the plate. "Well, I came out here to get Francisco, but there's something else on my mind." He looked at Hattie, Olive and then back to Brooks who sat down across from Hattie.

"Yes?"

"Tate Wilson at the telegraph office got word this morning. There are rumors going around about a gang that plans to kill every law officer they can find between here and Dallas. It came over the telegraph just this morning from Amarillo. Nobody knows where it started, but with Avila's gang on the rampage, we best be wary."

"That's a big stretch of road."

Olive's spoon clattered to the floor and Brooks picked it up to put it in her eager hand. "Ba ba, muk, muk," she babbled and opened her mouth for another spoonful of egg. Hattie spooned up another bite.

"Something else came over the telegraph from out of a little town in Louisiana. Morgan Ridge."

Hattie gasped; her face went pale. A choking sound came from her throat, but she clasped a hand over her mouth. "Coffee went down the wrong way," she sputtered.

"What did you hear?" Brooks asked, watching Hattie as she sat as still as stone, not daring to look up at Michael. The egg spilled from the spoon in her hand, but she didn't appear to notice.

"An orphanage there reported they'd had a baby stolen. Some woman came to the door, saying she'd been attacked by banditos. The matron there let her spend the night, and when she woke up, one of the babies was missing."

So that's where Olive came from!

Brooks glanced at Hattie from the corner of his eye. Her hands gripped white in her lap, and she shot him a look of stark fear as if compelling him not to give her away.

The sheriff tugged the collar of his blue shirt, clearly embarrassed to ask the obvious question, avoiding a direct look at either of them. "I guess – and I don't mean anything by this Brooks. It's just, Olive's description sounds like the baby missing from the orphanage. You tell me and I'll take your word, but I have to ask. Where did your baby come from?"

Realizing how that sounded, he blushed to the roots of his blond hair. "I mean ..." he stammered. "Is this Hattie's baby?"

"No need to be embarrassed, Michael," Brooks answered. "You're just doing your job. If I'd gotten a telegraph like that, I'd be questioning people too. And I guess it's we who should be embarrassed. Olive is ..."

Those green eyes bore into him, begging, pleading. *Oh, Hattie, how am I going to fix this for you?*

"Olive is ours. Hattie's and mine. I should have been honest with you from the start," he lied, knowing Michael would remember his story about Hattie coming to his door in Houma. Even as he told the untruth, he kept his eyes focused on Michael's. The sheriff's eyes widened. His mouth opened as if he meant to speak. Instead, he pursed his lips tight. An almost imperceptible nod of Michael's head told Brooks he understood. He would accept the lie – for now. Brooks hoped his relief at Michael's trust wasn't unfounded.

What am I saying? I'm taking up for a woman who stole a baby – me – the Golden Star. What has happened to my sense of right and wrong? Have I gotten so wrapped up in those green eyes and that captivating smile that I've lost my way?

"Then I'll take your word for it, and I won't ask any more questions."

I'm sure glad of that because more questions would require more lies. I need to get to the bottom of this first.

"Ma'am, I'm sorry if I've impugned your character." Michael stood, picked up his Stetson, and pushed in the kitchen chair. "Let me know when Francisco comes to, Brooks, or if you need any help here."

Brooks waved off any other words, waiting until they heard the wooden front door slam shut and the sound of Michael's horse riding away. Olive babbled and tapped her spoon. Outside, they heard Jeb calling to one of the barn cats.

Hattie wiped off Olive's sticky hands. "Thank you. I don't know what I'd have done if you took her away."

"Hattie," he sighed and sat down across from her. "I'm not sure telling him a lie was much better. What he must think of me with a young woman and a baby … It's indecent." He didn't let on that Michael knew he'd been lying. *Not yet.*

"Maybe so," she said staunchly, "but I don't care what he thinks of me. Olive was an orphan just like me, no folks of her own. What kind of a life would she have in a place like that orphanage? Why, that old matron had a wart on her nose as big as a grasshopper. Who wants to see that every morning? I just adopted her is all – just like any of those people who go get babies all the time."

"Not legally, Hattie. You stole her. You can't just steal a baby and get away with it."

Hattie sighed, lifted Olive out of the chair and clutched the baby protectively to her breast. "I didn't steal her. I give her a home and a family. Now she's mine."

"She doesn't belong to you. You took her. Why? Why would you steal a baby in the first place? I don't understand."

"Rafael told me to. He said I had to come to your house and say I'd been attacked. They said if I had a baby then I'd look more like a respectable woman. An' they said you weren't the kind of man who would turn your back on a baby."

"A woman with a baby but no husband hardly looks respectable."

"I was supposed to have a husband," Hattie argued, "a dead one. I just forgot that when you kept firing questions at me like you did." She looked at Olive, her eyes growing bright. "I want to adopt her for real. I don't want to give her back. I can't." As if Hattie couldn't quite believe the words or the emotions, she whispered with an incredulous expression in her eyes, "I love her."

Brooks stared at the two of them. Olive did seem to be bonding to Hattie, reaching her tiny hand up to tug at Hattie's lips. "Ma, ma," she babbled, "Ma, ma."

"Maybe we can figure out something," Brooks answered, feeling a deep hole in his own heart at the idea of not having Olive around. *I can't believe myself. I've lied to Michael, even if he knows it. I'm trying to think of a way to keep a baby stolen from an orphanage. What is happening to me?*

"I can keep her? You'll think of something, won't you?" Those green eyes shone with relief and confidence. "You won't let the sheriff take her back to the orphanage?"

He knew he would regret the promise. There could be only one right solution to this dilemma and Hattie would not like it. *Olive needs a home, a real family, but how can I refuse this woman anything she asks?*

If he hadn't known it before, he knew it then. *How did I manage to fall in love with this woman? Me, the Golden Star, in love with a woman bandito who stole a baby from an orphanage and wrapped herself around my heart? Oh, Lord, I'm in trouble now.*

"I'll think about it," he promised, ready to climb the highest mountain or ford the deepest stream to see those green eyes light up again like they did just then.

***

Later that night, Brooks stared down at the paper in his hand. He'd written three names six years ago after Mateo had been hanged. The other three members of Mateo's gang he hadn't caught. Mateo had boasted that he was the one who put the bullets through his wife and son's hearts, but the rest of the gang were just as responsible. They had pillaged his ranch, burnt his house, stolen his animals. They had not stopped Mateo in his evil carnage.

"What you reading?" Hattie asked as she walked by to check on Olive.

"It's the men who helped kill my family. Now that Francisco is in custody, there are only two. Edmundo and Frank."

"They're evil, just like Mateo, but Francisco, he's different. He wouldn't have had a hand in killing your family." Hattie stopped as if uncertain to share more, then blurted out. "They hate you for getting him hanged. They want revenge for him."

"Until today, I thought I wanted revenge too." He stared down at the worn paper in his hands. He'd held it so often it had grown soft from his touch. "Then I thought about Emily, my wife. She'd have been the first to say, *"Brooks, let God handle the revenge. You just do your job. You fight for justice."*

He looked up at Hattie and saw tears of sympathy glisten in her eyes. "I've hated these men for the past six years. Wanted them dead. Prayed for them to die. I didn't want justice.

"Justice isn't like revenge. Revenge is like vengeance, or a life for a life. Justice is letting the law decide, letting the truth come out. I didn't want the truth to come out – for those men to go free because a jury believed them."

"Well ..." Hattie moistened her lips as if unsure what to say.

Brooks went on speaking, working it out in his own mind. "Last night, when I went after Francisco and wanted to kill him, I had to ask myself. Did I want justice or revenge? And when I looked at myself real hard, I saw I wanted revenge. If, as you say, Francisco had no part in the actual killings, he should not hang for that. He should find justice – not *my* justice, but true justice."

"But you're the Golden Star," Hattie reminded him. "Mavi says people trust you to fight for justice."

"Maybe they did before. Now, I'm not sure they should. I'm not a lawman now, Hattie. If I seek revenge, doesn't that make me equal with Mateo's gang? I might as well be another member in a different gang. If I want revenge with a hatred as deep as theirs, then I'm not much different than they are. If I go after Edmundo and Frank, then I'm no better. I'm as much an animal as them."

Hattie shook her head. "That ain't true. You are a better man."

"You didn't think so yesterday, when I wanted to kill Francisco." He smiled dimly at the memory, those determined fists pounding his chest. *Stop that!* He wanted to shout at his heart for doing a fast flip and flop in his chest. *You can't love this woman. Look what happened to Emily when you loved her!*

Hattie blushed. "Well, I think so now. I think you need to catch those other two and stop them before anyone else gets killed. And there's something else you need to do. You better write down another name on that paper: Rafael Avila."

"He didn't kill my family. He didn't ride with Mateo."

"It don't matter. He's here now and he aims to kill you. He said you'll die on the same tree as Mateo, then true justice will be done. That's *his* justice. He brought you back here so you can watch his face, laughing as you die."

She looked into his eyes, silently willing him to understand. "If you don't kill Rafael first, you won't live to fight for any justice."

Chapter Twenty

"Please, let's go back to Louisiana," Hattie begged as she scurried behind Brooks as he did the evening chores. It had been a tense, watchful day after Sheriff Storey had gone back to Beaumont. By evening, Hattie's nerves were strung as tight as a barbed wire fence. Every time she looked out a window, she expected to see Rafael and the rest of the gang coming to kill them. She'd begun her pleading as soon as the supper dishes were washed and dried. "We can go back to Houma. You and me and Olive. Let Sheriff Storey deal with the gang. You don't have to do it. They killed *his* deputy."

"He was *my* friend." Brooks stopped to pitch a forked mound of hay into a cow's stall. "Sam wanted me to come back here to help Michael. I'm honor-bound to do it."

"No, he didn't!" Hattie argued, sidestepping past Jeb, who hurried past with a bucket of milk. "Rafael made him write that letter."

"No matter. It's still my duty."

"You did your duty years ago. Mavi told me. You caught Mateo after he rampaged around the town. Now it's Michael's turn. Let him deal with Rafael and his gang."

"I can't leave him alone to deal with this." Brooks walked to the haystack and scooped up more hay. He dropped it into the next cow's stall, giving the brown and white shorthorn a pat on the flank. Moving on to the next stall, he took up a shovel and started on the disagreeable chore of cleaning out the muck. "Hattie, I've got work to do. Why don't you go help Mavi awhile?"

Hattie grabbed his arm and clung tight. "I c-can't! I'm afraid. Rafael probably knows by now you caught Francisco.

If he thinks I've turned against him, none of us are safe here." She choked out a sob. "I don't want him to hurt Olive!"

"I won't let him hurt her," Brooks said, "or you."

"Please, let's just go back to Louisiana. Let's be safe."

Brooks finally stopped, put down the shovel and came to stand in front of her, taking hold of her arms. His hands felt warm and strong through the sleeves of her green dress. At his gentle touch, Hattie's heartbeat slowed. Suddenly, she wanted to lean against that broad chest, to whisper her fears close to his heart and have him hold her tight. His words, though spoken in a calm, reassuring way, did nothing to make her feel better. "We aren't safe anywhere. Rafael found me in Louisiana and sent you there. If we run now, we will never be safe anywhere. It's time to put a stop to the Avila's here and now."

"We can find somewhere else to be safe! Let's just leave, before Rafael finds us here."

"I can't go back to Louisiana. I've captured Francisco. Now I must capture Edmundo and Frank. Then I will help Michael round up the rest of the Avila gang."

"Oh, you!" Hattie jerked away. "I hope they do hang you! You're a darned fool!"

Fuming at Brooks, she stomped out of the barn and hurried toward the house. Although she knew it was probably just her fear, the land felt alive with eyes boring into her back. She strode across the dusty yard, heart thumping, breath racing. Even closing the solid wood door didn't make her feel safe enough.

Why didn't I just do like Rafael planned? Get Brooks Shanton back here to Texas. Why'd I have to get my heart all tangled up with him?

Inside the parlor, Olive toddled after her and Hattie picked her up. "You're a precious baby, you know that?"

The baby gurgled and patted Hattie's check. For the first time in a long time, Hattie thought of her mother. How had the woman done such a despicable thing – sold her to a gang? Had she a black heart? No feeling? Hattie knew she could never surrender Olive to anyone so vicious as Mateo had been.

"They won't ever take you." She hugged the baby tightly until Olive protested. "I promise you. I'm not like my Ma. I will never give up my daughter."

Daughter. This is my daughter. It was a new and frightening idea. "I will protect you. Swear by the stars in the sky. Nobody's gonna take you away from me."

Hattie wondered again about Olive. *How did you end up in an orphanage?* Must not have a Pa or Ma to be there – maybe lost her family to a fever or Indian attack or something. Not for the first time, Hattie wondered about what was supposed to happen to Olive after Rafael's plan.

"Was I supposed to just toss you aside? Forget how much I ... love you?"

Had Rafael planned for her to just drop Olive off at the orphanage? *Just dump her down on those cold, stone steps like a plaything or a puppy I didn't want.* "Not while I got breath in my body, baby."

In a little while, Brooks finished his chores and came in. On an impulse, Hattie lifted Olive and held her toward him. "Take her, Brooks. Hold her."

Brooks reached out for the baby and held her tenderly, smiling down at her and planting a kiss on her blonde curls.

146

"You're a sweet girl, aren't you?" Olive gurgled and giggled, patted his cheek, and reached back for Hattie.

"This could be our family," Hattie whispered. "We could be a real family."

"Hattie," Brooks said with regret in his voice, "it wouldn't work out. Olive needs a real family. A family might have found her if you'd left her at the orphanage. A family with a mother and a father."

"No, listen. I don't know why Olive was in that orphanage. Maybe her family died or maybe somebody just didn't want her. Maybe her Ma was like mine and gave her up. I don't reckon I'll ever know. But I can protect her. She can be mine, and yours too, like you told that Sheriff.

"You can love her and make a life for her!" She wanted to add *and me* but kept quiet, watching him hold the baby, a smile on his lips. "Instead of taking revenge on the Avilas, you could take us back to Louisiana."

Brooks shook his head and walked away. Tears pooled in Hattie's eyes, but she pressed her lips tight and said nothing else.

***

Brooks walked to the bedroom where Francisco lay handcuffed to the iron bed. He knocked and Jeb came to the door. "How's he doing?"

Jeb shook his head. "Not too well at present. Mavi came in and dressed the wound again a while ago. I told her to go on home and get some rest. As soon as I make sure he still asleep for the night, I'm gonna go home too. She said he's got a high fever. If it breaks, he be okay. If not … Nothing else we can do for him."

Brooks stared at the bandito. *It would be so easy to just shoot him now. To get revenge for his part in Emily and the boys' deaths.* But Hattie's determined stance and those glaring green eyes came to his mind. The angry words she'd shouted at him to keep him from killing Francisco yesterday.

"You ain't no different than them. You hate just as bad. You kill and say it's justice."

He couldn't deny she'd been right. "Has he regained consciousness at all?"

Jeb shook his head, a mournful expression on his dark face. "Here and there. He mumbles a lot about Rafael and you. He's powerful angry at you, Mister Brooks."

"I sure wish he'd come to, so I could question him. So I'd know Rafael's plans. According to Hattie, he wants revenge for Mateo. If Francisco wakes, he could give me vital information."

"If he would, "Jeb answered. "Might be he'd rather not help you. I keep wonderin' if he's the one who killed Mister Sam. I know the Good Book says we gotta forgive, but I'm finding it awful hard when I think of Mister Sam. He was a good man."

"That he was. Why don't you go home for the night, Jeb? I'll sit here a bit. He's not going anywhere."

Jeb went home and Brooks sat by Francisco's bedside for a while. Darkness came and he sat on, thinking of what Hattie had said when she'd placed Olive in his arms. *I would like a real family again. I can't deny my feelings for Hattie either, but how can I even think about loving a woman again? What if, because of me, she dies – like Emily did? It wouldn't be fair to love again … but, oh, how I wish I could!*

He let his thoughts drift as he listened to Francisco's ragged breathing and low groans. Staring at the man's greasy, pock-marked face, he wondered what led someone to a life such as the Avilas had. Why hate so much?

After another few minutes, Brooks left Francisco handcuffed to the bed and headed upstairs. He walked past Hattie's room. The door was open, as if she had been waiting for him, the dim light from the oil lamp on the dresser spilling into the hall. As he walked by, she ran out and clutched his arm. The sight of her in the long, white nightgown took his breath away. *Oh, Hattie, why'd you have to go and wrap yourself around my heart?*

'Please," she begged, squeezing his arm, her green eyes filled with hope, "sit with me. I'm afraid."

"There's nothing to be afraid of. I'm here."

"Please?" Hattie held tight to his arm and pulled him into the bedroom. "Watch over me while I sleep. I ain't never done anything like this before, but I'm afraid that they'll come for you, and I won't be able to fend them off. They'll hurt Olive. Or me."

She motioned toward the crib Mavi had found and placed in a corner of the room. A ragged sob shook her body. "I don't want them to hurt her." As if she didn't quite know how to express her feelings, Hattie shuddered, and the words came out in a torrent. "I ain't never loved anyone like I love her. Maybe you don't believe me, but it's true. She's my daughter as much as if I'd birthed her."

"I believe you, Hattie."

"Then please stay with me so I don't need to be afraid. So no one hurts her. Please!"

"There's no call to be afraid." Brooks pulled the rocking chair near the foot of the bed. "I'll sit here and watch over you through the night."

"You will?" she asked in a tremulous voice, as if she couldn't believe it. In her long white nightgown, her short blond hair beginning to curl at the ends, she looked nearly like an angel. Brooks had to look away when he found himself staring hungrily at her face, those moist lips, and wondering how it would feel to kiss a woman again.

No, not just any woman. I want to kiss Hattie.

Brooks pulled the rocking chair near the foot of the bed and sat down. "You go on to sleep. I'll be here. You're safe."

"You promise?" After he nodded, Hattie lay down on the bed and pulled the yellow and orange crazy quilt up to her chin. She lay still for a minute, then raised her head to whisper, "You won't go away? You promise?"

"I promise."

He waited until he heard her steady breathing before he got up and blew out the lamp. For a minute, he stood over the bed looking down at her. Before he could stop himself, he put a gentle hand on her cheek and brushed a lock of hair away from her eyes. *It would be so easy to love her ...*

It took every ounce of his will to sit back down in the rocking chair. To tighten his hands around the wooden chair arms and plant his feet firmly on the floor. *Loving her would be wrong. She wouldn't be safe if she loved me. Just like Emily wasn't safe. I'm the one who caused Emily's death with my righteousness, my striving for justice. My fault ... all ... my ... fault ...*

He must have dozed off or just closed his eyes when a low moan startled him awake. Hattie cried out, "No, no!"

Brooks was alert and up in an instant, sitting beside her on the bed. He wrapped his arm around her shoulders as if it were the most natural thing in the world, grabbing her flailing arms and holding them in his warm, strong hands. To still her weeping, he held her close and patted her back as if she were Olive's age. "Shush, shush, it's okay, you're just having a bad dream. Don't be afraid, don't be afraid," he murmured.

"I was so scared," she wept, leaning into his shoulder, clutching his arms tight, her warm face pressed against his chest. Her tears wet the front of his brown shirt. "They were coming for me, and I couldn't get away. I couldn't save Olive. They were gonna take her like they took the little rabbit. Don't let them get her!"

"Sh, sh, they won't get Olive. I won't let them." He could feel her heart beating against his chest. Hattie lifted her face, just inches from his and looked up into his eyes. *Those green eyes.* He felt as if he were drowning in the depths of them. *I love you. Oh, Hattie, how did I not know until now? Or did I know and not want to believe it could be true?*

"Hattie," he whispered, aware of her body pressed against his, the warmth of her and the sweetness of her sleep-flushed face. "Hattie Munn ..." His voice caught in his throat as he tried to express everything he felt and knowing he would fail as a surge of emotion rose to capture his heart. "Did anyone ever tell you what a beautiful woman you are?"

He thought her lips mumbled *no* – but he didn't wait for her answer. His lips came down on hers. So soft, so pliable, so sweet beneath his lips. A soft scent surrounded him – like rainwater and lavender – and he kissed her again. Something in his mind told him to stop, to leave. "I want ..." He knew what he wanted, but something stopped him. This woman, this girl in his arms had been abused, treated like a plaything. Could he dishonor her too? Would it be right to take advantage of her need for love? *Or mine?* "I want to ..."

Gunfire shattered the window beside the bed.

Chapter Twenty-One

Gunfire tore through the night as a rain of glass shards sprinkled down on the bed and floor. Brooks scrambled away, with Hattie tucked into the crook of his arm. Another bullet crashed through the window and plunked into the wall. A volley of gunfire pierced a destructive pattern on the flowered wallpaper, shattering the dresser mirror. Hattie screamed, and Olive's piercing cry ripped through the darkness.

"Olive!" Hattie tried to jerk out of Brooks' grasp, intent on rushing to the baby's crib.

"Stay down!" Brooks ordered, shouting over another storm of bullets. "Crawl and get her. Then take her into the hall."

Brooks grabbed his gun and, standing by the side of the window, sent off a volley of return shots from his Colt 45. The banditos outside returned his fire.

"Stay down!" he repeated. Olive's shrieks of terror rose louder.

Another bullet pierced the oil lamp and shattered the design of yellow roses and vines. The glass fragments littered the floor, but Hattie crawled through them as if they were grass.

"Hattie," Brooks cautioned, torn between protecting her and letting those outside know they had a fight, "your hands! You're bleeding."

"It's them!" Hattie screamed. "They won't let us leave." She jerked the baby from the crib and cradled her against her chest, leaving bloody handprints on both Olive's white nightgown and her own. "We're all going to die. I couldn't save Olive; I couldn't save her," she cried.

"Hattie, listen to me! Take Olive and get to the stairs. Go to the kitchen. I'm going to get Francisco and take him to the back. We can try to get to the Jacksons' cabin."

As if she didn't hear, Hattie sat on the floor, rocking the baby back and forth in her lap, sobbing. Olive kept on screaming, her voice rising in pitch each time another bullet pierced through the windows. Brooks sent another couple of shots out the window, knowing he'd have to reload before he could attempt it again.

"Hattie, listen!" He hurried to her, pulled her to her feet and together they stumbled out into the relative safety of the hallway. Hattie sobbed but leaned against him as he led them down the stairs. Olive clung to Hattie's nightgown, a pathetic little bundle of misery. "We're going to get out of this," Brooks tried to reassure Hattie, but she had gone someplace inside herself and kept moaning, almost as if she'd given up. Brooks shook her hard. "Listen to me! Can you crawl to the kitchen?"

"We're going to die," Hattie moaned. "Die! They won't let us leave."

Knowing there was no way to trust Hattie in her present state, Brooks led her and a whimpering Olive to the kitchen.

If we can get outside to the Jackson's cabin, or get some horses ...

As they hurried through the small hallway between the kitchen and the parlor, Brooks stole a glance out the window. Shadows of men and horses circled the barn, and a flaming torch flew towards the Jackson's cabin. *There goes that plan.* Brooks could only spare a grateful thought that the Jacksons were not home. The wooden shingles of the roof blazed up like they'd been splashed with coal oil, and the pungent odor sifting through the night air told him he'd guessed right.

He used precious seconds to place Hattie and Olive in the space behind the big Franklin stove, the safest place he could think of. "Stay down! I'll be right back. I'm going to get Francisco." He hurried into the bedroom, keeping away from the windows. Already the flickering light from the flames outside made the room bright as sunrise.

"Francisco!"

The man, startled by the gunfire, struggled weakly against the restraints. "*Que*? What's happening?" he mumbled.

Brooks unlocked the handcuffs and dragged the man off the bed, holding his Colt in one hand. He managed to pull the barely-conscious man into his right arm and against his shoulder, half carrying, half dragging him through the hall to the kitchen. He shoved Francisco under the kitchen table, where he might be shielded from exploding glass and shattering dishes. There wasn't much chance of him getting away with a busted leg, but Brooks didn't want any of the other banditos to try to rescue him. If they survived the night, Francisco might be their only hope of finding Rafael.

"Keep an eye on him," he told Hattie over Olive's shrieks of terror. "I'm going to check out the front windows."

Hattie didn't speak a word, but her eyes – those lovely green eyes – stared at him in despair. Silent sobs shook her body as she clung to the baby.

"I will keep you safe. I promise you."

Just like you kept Emily safe, his mind taunted. *Hattie will die too. You can't keep her safe.*

From the front windows, Brooks' worst nightmare came to life. Like the fires from an inferno, he watched Sam's barn burst into the fiery orange outline of a building. Corral fences were nothing but broken splinters of wood. The banditos had at least had the decency to let the horses out of the corral; they galloped away from the burning barn as a wide-eyed cow ran past in panic, a flock of chickens scattering before it like leaves in the wind. Brooks saw several men on horses, heard their whooping and frantic hollering, like savages on a warpath. The pungent odor of coal oil and kerosene assaulted his nose as a man rode by and splashed the front porch liberally.

Brooks took the time to scrabble through Sam's gun rack, pulling down a Winchester and another Colt revolver. Brooks yanked the drawer beneath the cabinet open and took a deep, steadying breath as he loaded his weapons using the boxes of ammunition inside. His hands were sure and steady, even as his heart pounded with fear.

Once the guns were loaded, he went to a window, broke it with the gun barrel, and fired out. He knew he couldn't hit anything, not with the shadows and flames making a target impossible. *Just so you know I'm here and I'm fighting.*

He ran back into the kitchen. Olive had stopped shrieking but continued to emit shuddering sobs against Hattie's white nightgown. Hattie sat motionless behind the stove, eyes staring wide. Another volley of bullets pelted the kitchen cabinets and Olive shrieked again as Brooks ducked.

Brooks had never felt so helpless. He laid the extra guns on the kitchen table and filled the pockets of his trousers with extra ammunition. *How am I going to keep them safe? How can I protect them?* It seemed a strange time to do it, but Brooks knew he had to say what he'd been trying to ignore for too long, what he'd known tonight as he took Hattie in his arms for the first time.

"Hattie," he knelt beside her, one hand holding his revolver and the other wrapped around her and Olive, then whispered in her ear, "I love you. I can't help myself. I love you."

Even with the gunfire and the flickering light from the flames rising out of the night, Hattie's face took on a luminous glow. Those haunted green eyes stared at him, and she gasped. For just a moment, the shouts and frantic animals bawling and squawking outside seemed to still, and he heard her sweet, soft reply: "I think I love you too."

Brooks knew they both might die that night, perhaps even in the next few minutes, but he wanted her to know his heart. A horse whinnied frantically outside and Olive's baby screams didn't diminish, but Brooks leaned down and kissed Hattie on the lips. How sweet her lips felt beneath his! He kissed her again and pressed her as close as he could with Olive between them. "We need to get out of here," he whispered. "I'm going to try to catch a couple of horses."

She nodded, but he saw the fear in her eyes. A timid hand came up to touch his lips with her gentle fingers. In her eyes, he saw the hopelessness of it all.

"I will come back to you."

Another doomed nod, as if nothing in her life had ever gone right and she didn't believe it ever would.

"You keep watch over Francisco." He reached for the extra Colt and handed it to her. "Can you use a gun?" She nodded. "Good! If you need to use it …"

Don't let her have to use it! I can't lose her like I lost Emily and the boys.

Brooks went to the kitchen door, gave her a smile, and darted out, shooting as he went. A cascade of shots aimed at him, but he ducked behind the horse's water trough, belly to the ground. The bullets pinged into wood and the metal of a downspout, and he saw a puff of dirt from the ground. Sam's sow and her piglets raced past him, squealing in terror.

"Avila!" he called, certain he knew who was out there. "Avila!

More gunfire. Someone threw a flaming torch toward the trough, but it dropped into the water and fizzled out. Brooks crawled along the dusty ground and hid behind a wagon wheel. The Jacksons' cabin had fallen into ash and charred ruins. The night was as bright as day as fires crackled through the barn, the haystacks …

As he watched in horror, a rider approached the house and tossed a lighted torch on the kerosene-soaked porch. While the stucco and red clay tiles of the roof would not burn, the pinon wood the porch was made from surely would. It ignited with a *woosh,* sweeping devastation into the parlor.

Hattie! Olive!

Brooks turned, unmindful of Avila or his gang, his eyes on the porch. The walls might not burn, but the parlor windows burst from the intense heat, and he watched in helpless fury as the curtains and rocking chairs ignited. Flames shot upward into the blackness of the night, licking holes in the porch roof, bursting out what glass hadn't shattered from the gunfire.

Cursing, Brooks took aim at a man galloping by on a horse. He knew he hit the man, but it must not have been a fatal wound, as the rider tossed another flaming torch to the porch and rode away.

"Avila! You …!" No curse he could think of seemed powerful enough. Brooks kept his head down and made his way across the barnyard to the house. *If anything happened to Hattie or Olive …*

Across the valley, Brooks heard the unmistakable sound of gunfire.

Suddenly, from the direction of town, Michael Storey and a group of men galloped toward the ranch. They traded gunfire with the banditos, driving them to retreat past the barn. Brooks had never felt such a surge of gratitude in his life.

"You better surrender!" Michael hollered as he charged into the barnyard. "You're surrounded."

Even Brooks saw they were far from surrounding the group of shadowy banditos he saw in the orange glow from the flames, but just as suddenly as they'd arrived, the banditos rode into a tight formation and bolted away. Michael and part of his men headed after the group to give chase.

Brooks was sure the banditos would give them the slip somehow. Mateo Avila had been like an evil wraith who could vanish in the night. There was no reason to doubt his brother, Rafael, wouldn't do the same.

"You, men," a voice called out, "let's try to save what we can! Someone grab something to fight this fire."

They scurried to beat out the flames with feed stacks they wet in the horse trough. One man set up a bucket brigade from the large holding tank beneath the windmill and other men hurried to get in line to toss the water on the sizzling flames. The night filled with an acrid, burning stench that pierced the nose and burned the eyes.

Brooks hurried toward the house. Before his feet hit the kitchen porch, Hattie came through the door, coughing from the black smoke, her face wet with tears. The baby in her arms had finally stopped crying, but the terror etched on Olive's little face tore Brooks' heart in two.

"Are you hurt? Is Olive?"

Hattie couldn't answer, just kept shaking her head. When Brooks tried to pull Olive into his arms, the baby clung tighter to Hattie and buried her face against Hattie's bloody, soot-covered nightgown.

"Anyone else inside?" someone asked.

"A wounded captive under the kitchen table," Brooks managed to answer. The man, whoever he was, hurried to rescue Francisco and drag him out of the house, coughing and choking on the black smoke.

Brooks stopped and looked around at the ranch Sam had loved. As he watched, the last of the barn's beams crashed into an enormous pile of burning wood, shooting sparks and flames. The remains of the Jacksons' cabin lay smoldering in ash. Most of the corral fences had been reduced to jagged fragments of wood or burning piles of posts. Animals bawled and squawked; a few horses trotted past to safety.

The house appeared as though it would stay standing, but the flames and gunfire had done a world of damage. Most of the windows were shattered, and gunfire had shredded the walls, curtains, and even some of the furniture. Black smoke poured from the parlor windows as the men from town tried to save some of the furniture Sam had cherished.

I'm sorry, Sam.

As Brooks went to put his arm around Hattie, one of the deputies came riding back. "Sheriff Storey said to tell you he's going to keep tracking them for a while," the man said as he reined in his horse near Brooks. "They gave us the slip and we can't tell which direction they went. He said to come back and give you this." The man leaned down to hand Brooks a rock wrapped with a piece of parchment and tied with twine. The words Golden Star were visible, scrawled on the outside of the parchment.

As Hattie clung tight to his arm, Brooks untied the twine and read the note written on the paper out loud to Hattie.

"*Sheriff Shanton – You will come in three days to the place drawn on this map. Then we will have a final showdown and justice will be done. Rafael Avila.*"

Beside him, cradled into his right arm, Hattie wept.

Chapter Twenty-Two

It was the longest night Brooks could remember. Neighbors came from nearby ranches, alerted by the glow of the fire, to help. Some women Brooks had never met took Hattie and Olive under their capable, calico-covered arms. Hattie's cuts were bandaged, and Olive was soothed and put back to sleep on a pallet in an army tent. More women brought food and coffee to help the men still attempting to douse the smoldering ruins of Sam's house. They carried out furniture, bedding, dishes, anything still deemed salvageable. Francisco had been placed in another tent someone had erected near a wagon. Others had taken the horses and built a crude corral at a distance from the flames. Animals were rescued and penned. Any grain or hay still viable had been recovered. The neighbors worked to restore anything they could to help – the same as they knew Sam would have helped them in a time of crisis.

At some point in the long night, Michael rode back into the barnyard with the disappointing news that Avila and his gang had evaded them.

"I'm sorry, Brooks." Michael accepted a cup of hot coffee and a sandwich from one of the ministering women. "We trailed them at least ten miles but they slipped away."

Brooks told him the contents of the note on the rock.

"What do you plan to do?" Michael asked.

"Meet him and end this," Brooks answered, staring off at Hattie, who was sitting near the army tent where Olive slept. "One way or another. This killing and destruction must stop. I've been running from this too long. Now it's time to face up to it."

Toward dawn, as the chilly, smoke-scented night ended, Jeb and Mavi rode in with Father Kemp to view the devastation. Mavi wept openly, falling to the ground with her face in the dirt. "We ain't got nothin' left. Nothin'. Who could be so evil?"

Although Jeb's face wore a stoic look of acceptance, Brooks could see a glint of tears in his dark eyes, too. There was nothing to say, no way to comfort them. After a while, Mavi went to sit beside Hattie and put her arm around the younger woman. Jeb just stood and stared. Silent. After a time of mourning, he walked through the ruins until he found a bucket, picked it up and went to find any grain or hay he could to feed the pigs and chickens.

As the pink ribbons of sunrise swept away the shreds of night, the neighbors left, one after the other. There would be morning chores waiting for them at home after a long, sleepless night. Brooks had met most of Sam's neighbors in the past, and he tried to speak a word of thanks to everyone as they said goodbye.

Michael and his men headed back to town, leaving a deputy behind to help guard Francisco.

"I'd take him back to town with me," Michael told Brooks, "but I must think, if Avila knew he was here, he would have tried to rescue him. Now that they've done their worst to Sam's ranch, I don't think they will even suspect he's here or try to come back. You're probably safer than we will be in town."

"He's my only chance to find out what Avila plans. Once I'm able to question him, I can get more information from him."

"What makes you think he'll tell you anything?" Michael asked as he mounted his stallion to leave. The horse pawed at the ground, anxious to ride away.

Brooks clenched his jaw. "He will tell me."

The sun rose in the east to a scene of absolute devastation – or so it seemed to Brooks. Standing beside a small campfire the women had made to heat coffee, he held a tin mug clenched in both hands. He had yet to take a sip. Eating and drinking seemed like useless chores just then. He placed the mug down on a log. Despite the glowing rays of the sun, warming the earth and shining beacons of light over the smoldering ruins, Brooks' eyes saw only dark clouds.

The only bright spot in the morning was Hattie. Someone had brought clean clothes and Hattie now wore a deep burgundy dress patterned with dark feathers. It suited her, and Brooks' breath caught in his throat at the womanly shape of her body. *If I had lost her last night ... My Hattie – my beautiful Hattie.*

She came to stand beside him and reached out to touch his arm. The palms of her hands were bandaged with white linen. As she reached for him, he lifted one of her wounded hands and kissed the top of the bandage. "I'm sorry."

"It don't hurt much," Hattie murmured, her eyes haunted by an inner pain. "Someone put salve on the cuts. I'm just thankful Olive didn't get hurt." After a few silent minutes, she whispered in a quivery voice, "Or you."

At that moment, it felt like the most natural thing in the world to pull her close to him and shelter her in his arms, her face pressed to the chest of his sooty dark blue shirt. When she glanced up at him, so trusting, he gave her a stricken look and gently kissed her forehead. "I'm sorry. I feel like I've failed everything and everyone. Last night I was afraid I'd lose you and Olive." He held her tighter, feeling her heartbeat, warm and comforting against his chest. "I failed Sam. He trusted me to come help him and I couldn't prevent his death."

"You tried to get here," Hattie interrupted but Brooks shook his head, eyes dark with pain.

"I didn't make it in time. Now, I've let Avila's gang destroy everything Sam loved. I've caused the Jacksons to lose their home and their livelihoods. Everything is gone. There's nothing left."

Hattie lifted her face up to stare straight into his eyes. "That ain't so. There is something left – none of us got hurt last night. We're all still here."

"Hattie ..."

"No, you listen." Those green eyes snapped, and she grasped both his arms like an angry schoolmarm. "This morning, me and Mavi went out to look at the garden."

Brooks shook his head. He, too, had walked out to look at the garden plot Hattie had so proudly told him she'd help plant. The banditos had trampled all the fine little tomato plants, crushed them under the hooves of their horses, and it nearly broke his heart. It was almost as if they'd crushed Hattie, once again, under their boots. Brooks had grieved for her.

"Me an Mavi was remembering how hot it was when we planted them. And I was thinking ..." she blushed but took a deep breath and squeezed his arms as tight as she could in the clumsy bandages. "I was remembering how I thought maybe those tomatoes would grow and I'd feed you and Olive. Now they're all gone – all wilted and dying. I cried. Sure enough, I cried, but then Mavi set me straight.

164

"She said, '*Well, there ain't no use cryin', Miss Hattie. They's jes' things. We can plant more tomatoes and another crop will grow. We can replace plants, so they ain't real important. It's the people you can't replace. Me and Jeb might have lost our home, but we still have each other and the gumption to start over. Long as we got us, we ain't lost everything.*'"

As if wanting to make sure he understood her, Hattie stuck out her chin defiantly and stood up on tiptoes to make herself taller. "Just 'cause the tomatoes and the ranch are mostly gone don't mean we have to give up. It don't mean *you* have to give up. I never knew your friend, Sam, but I think he'd be right proud you tried to help, an' I think he'd know you tried to save everything. He'd be glad you got the gumption to go after Rafael and the others."

"Where did you learn to be so wise?" he whispered down at her earnest face, his heart leaping in a crazy way as he stared into the depths of those green eyes. "Sam would be the first to say something like, '*Don't be a confounded fool, Brooks. Don't cry over spilled milk. Wipe it up and move on.*'"

"I reckon I learned some of what Mavi knows," Hattie answered honestly. "'Cause I been mostly dumb my whole life, not having any schooling or such. But, I think she's right. If we got each other, then we're gonna come out fine. I'm sorry about your friend, Sam, and your ..." Hattie hesitated but then her voice grew stronger, "your wife and your family. I never knew them, but I think they'd know you tried to help an' did your best. Just 'cause your best wasn't altogether good enough, don't mean you got to blame yourself. Mateo killed them, not you."

Brooks was stunned by her wisdom. Through the years since Emily's death, he had wrestled with the notion that if he hadn't let his stubborn refusal to be intimidated rule his life, Emily might still be alive. Listening to Hattie, he realized a deeper truth: to have stopped being the Golden Star would have been wrong. Emily would have been the first person to tell him that. Sam would've been the second.

The tight fist that clasped his heart the past six years eased open. For the first time in a long, long time, he looked ahead without heartache. He knew, deep inside, that both his wife and old deputy would have told him he needed to be true to his ideals.

"Thank you, sweet Hattie," he whispered and buried his face in her sun-warmed hair. "I love you."

"What are you going to do now?"

"Meet Avila like he asks. It's time to end this. The people of Beaumont have suffered long enough. Sam's death needs to be avenged." Hattie scowled until he began to explain. "Rafael and the rest of the gang need to be brought to justice. For all the people they have killed. For the things they've done to you and the people in Beaumont. Justice needs to be served, Hattie. People shouldn't have to live in fear."

She sighed.

Bending down to plant a kiss on her short, rumpled hair, he whispered, " I have to be true to what I know, Hattie, or I'm worth nothing."

"I wish ... well, I don't rightly know what I wish. I know what Rafael is capable of, an' I know he wants you dead. I'm afraid for you."

He smiled, and tried to reassure her. "There's nothing to be afraid about. We've still got Francisco. He knows more about what Rafael plans than we do. If I can talk to him, we have hope we can get the jump on Rafael."

Hattie's skepticism showed on her face, those rosy lips pursed in doubt. Her eyes narrowed with suspicion. "What makes you think Francisco will tell you anything?"

"Hattie ..." Before he could form an answer, she surprised him with a blurted remark that took his breath away.

"Let's get married, today, before I lose you."

"Married?"

"Yes, now, today. Father Kemp can marry us. He's a *Padre* – can't he do it? Please, Brooks, please? Last night you said you loved me. I love you, too. Don't you want to marry me? Or were you just lying last night when you said you loved me? Ain't that what people do when they love each other?"

Brooks shook his head and pulled her closer. "Oh, Hattie, I do love you. I do want to marry you, but look what happened to Emily when I married her. I don't want to lose you too, Hattie."

"Then marry me, today!" Hattie's face turned up to him and she trembled in his arms. "I don't want to lose you either, Brooks. When you meet Rafael, if ..."

She didn't have to spell out her fear as her eyes took on a hunted look. Brooks felt the blood pulse in his throat and a cold fist closed over his heart. *If this is the only thing I can give her ... If Rafael wins ... I can't deny her this.*

If I should die ...

Chapter Twenty-Three

Father Kemp took the news philosophically with a gentle smile on his lips. "Are you a Catholic, my dear?" he asked Hattie.

"No," Hattie answered in almost a wail, clutching Brooks' hand like a little girl about to be denied her heart's desire. "Do I gotta be? I will if I gotta be – but I don't know how."

The priest smiled kindly, "Well, that's no matter. If I recall correctly, Brooks was a churchgoer many years ago."

"A long time ago," Brooks answered, "but if you can see fit to marry us, Father, I'd be mighty obliged."

Father Kemp talked to them for a while. Brooks watched Hattie's eyes, trying to understand as the priest spoke to them about the duties of married life and how they must love and care for one another during the good times and the bad. *Sweet Hattie, who's probably never known anyone who's been married.* Brooks couldn't stop watching her face as she stared intently at the priest, biting her lip as if she wanted to make sure she understood, clutching his hand with her bandaged ones like a little girl who needed protection.

Finally, Father Kemp nodded and went to his saddlebags for his missal. "I think we can proceed whenever you're ready."

The ceremony was small, with just Brooks, Hattie, and the Jacksons to stand as witnesses. The deputy watching over Francisco's tent and Olive were the only others present, though Olive found more delight in chasing chickens than in watching the wedding.

Mavi insisted on making a wedding lunch with supplies the neighbors had brought the night before. After eating lunch,

Father Kemp blessed them all and left for town. Later, Brooks had no idea what he'd eaten. It all tasted like sawdust, and he could see Hattie seemed to have the same trouble swallowing anything. Every few minutes she would peek at him, then flush red and turn her attention back to Olive.

After lunch, Brooks and Jeb took care of some of the ranch chores while Mavi and Hattie fixed up one of the army tents as a bedroom. Brooks found himself anticipating the evening as a tide of joy washed over him. Maybe Hattie was right; maybe they *could* be happy. His thoughts would sail away on clouds of happiness then come crashing back down when he thought of Rafael Avila. *Tomorrow, I may die.* Several times, Jeb had to nudge him to pay attention to his work.

"I reckon's you got a right to seem wobbly-headed today, Mister Brooks," Jeb said after Brooks accidentally tipped over the milk pail. It surprised Brooks that Jeb could tease, despite losing his home and everything the night before, but Jeb set him straight with a reminder much like Hattie's earlier. "Reckon we got to snatch what happy we can and go right on livin'. Lestwise, none of us got killed last night. Got to rejoice in that, Mister Brooks."

It felt like the longest day he'd ever lived and doubts kept creeping in. How would Hattie feel about a wedding night? She had been abused by the gang for so long; would she be afraid? Trusting? As joyful as he felt? If this were to be their only night together ... Brooks didn't want to think about that.

Mavi offered to take Olive for the night. She and Jeb had managed to tie a tarp to the side of a wagon and make a small lean-to near the animal pens.

Hattie was already in bed – if pallets on the ground could be called a bed – when Brooks entered the tent. He swallowed a lump in his throat and felt like a schoolboy fidgeting in his boots. Easing off his suspenders, he started to unbutton his shirt.

"Hattie …" He wanted to tell her that he understood if she wanted to wait for a wedding night. *If her years of abuse have spoiled her for real love, I won't take advantage of her tonight. I can wait but, Oh, Lord it will be a trial.*

But Hattie left him in no doubt. She lifted the edge of the yellow and orange quilt, rescued from Sam's house, and asked in a sweet, though timid voice, "Aren't you coming to bed?"

"Are you sure?"

Those lovely green eyes held a little trepidation; she bit the corner of her lip, but she nodded and managed to put on a slight smile. "I love you; Brooks and I don't want to lose you."

It was the only invitation he needed.

***

Hattie rode into Beaumont the next morning with Jeb, Olive on the saddle before her. The cuts on her hands were healing, so she'd left off part of the linen bandages. She had to hold the reins gingerly in the tips of her fingers, but had no problems riding.

This morning she'd come to a decision, with Brooks' agreement. She was taking Olive to Father Kemp.

"I don't know what will happen when you meet Rafael," Hattie said that morning as they lay in one another's arms, "but I don't want her to be hurt. If … if something happens to you – or to us – I want Olive safe and protected."

Brooks kissed her neck and murmured into her hair. "It might be best. We can't expect the Jacksons to take care of her. But I hope you aren't thinking of going along when I meet Rafael. It's not going to happen, Hattie."

That's what you think.

"I mean it, Hattie. Rafael is a dangerous man."

I know. I've lived with him since I was thirteen. "I know that, but I'd feel safer with Olive in town. Could I take her in to Father Kemp? Please? Jeb is riding in with some of the neighbors – the Marshalls – so we'd be safe enough."

Brooks had agreed after a while, reluctantly pulling himself off the pallet and yanking on his pants. "Make sure Jeb takes a gun. And Hattie – maybe you had best take a Colt too. I'm going to try to convince Francisco to help us."

***

"How are you this morning?" the priest's eyes twinkled as she stepped into the cool darkness of the adobe church, filled with the scent of incense and beeswax. Four rows of wooden pews lined the inside, and near the front, candles flickered before an altar. Hattie recognized the statues as Jesus and Mary from visits with Mateo and Rafael. The Avilas had often gone into churches to pray – an idea Hattie had never quite fathomed. *Does God really listen to them? Thieves and murderers?*

The priest spoke again, and she realized she hadn't answered him. "What brings you into my church, Mrs. Shanton? I see you've brought little Olive for a visit."

Mrs. Shanton. Now doesn't that sound fine!

Hattie thought of Brooks last night and blushed, looking away from the priest's too-knowing smile. She set Olive down on the red tile bricks of the church floor. The baby toddled down the aisle, peeking into the empty pews. As if she knew she were in a holy place, Olive's baby prattle hushed. "Ma ma, muk, muk."

"Brooks will make a fine father to your child. Mavi explained the … um … circumstances of the baby's birth."

Hattie had no idea what Mavi knew or had told, but if the priest wanted to think of her as a wayward woman, he was probably right glad he'd got her married proper the day before. No way did Hattie plan to tell a priest where Olive had really come from. Probably best he never knew, especially if he agreed to her request.

"I'm right fine, Father Kemp. I brought Olive in because – well, I guess you know Brooks plans to meet Rafael tomorrow."

"Yes, it was my first prayer this morning. For years, I have buried or consoled one side or the other. I comforted and prayed with Brooks when his wife and sons were murdered. Rafael himself paid a visit to light a candle for his brother, Mateo. For too many years, this church has stood in the middle of hate and violence. The fighting must stop, or we will never be whole again." His brown robe swished across the tiles as he walked toward the front of the church. A young boy in a long black and white dress stood near the altar. "Thad, you can leave now," the priest called out. "Remind your mother I will need her help with the altar linens later, please."

The boy nodded and hurried behind the altar.

"Now, what was it you wanted?"

"Can you take Olive and keep her?" Hattie glanced at her baby and her heart clenched like it might break in two. "Promise me if I don't come back, if something happens to Brooks an' me that you'll find her a good home?"

"You, my dear? Surely you don't plan to become involved in this fight."

Hattie stood taller. "I got to, Father. I know Rafael and what he's capable of doing. If Brooks is going to face him, then I have to help him. The Avilas took my Ma and me, and other people. I won't let them have Brooks. Not while I got breath in my body."

The priest shook his head, a frown creased his weathered face and worry furrowed his forehead. "I can see how much you love him, Hattie, but I've known Brooks Shanton a long time. I can't see him allowing you to help."

"Please, just keep Olive here and promise you will find her a good home, a loving home, if we don't survive. I can't give her much, but if you promise, I can give her that."

Hattie didn't know if she had convinced the priest. He kept staring at her with an anxious look in his eyes. Maybe he needed a few minutes to pray on it. Hattie watched him turn his face to the altar, close his eyes and finally turn back to her. "I promise. I will take her to Mrs. Harrison; she's Thad's mother and a very good woman. Olive will be safe until you return."

If we return ...

Olive, still busy peeking in and out of the pews, didn't notice Hattie hurrying down the red tiled floor. It was all Hattie could do not to look back. Hardening her heart, she kept walking even as Olive finally did notice and questioned, "Ma ma?"

Father Kemp followed her to the heavy wooden doors and held up a hand in blessing. "Go with God."

Only if God sides with us and not Rafael.

Olive's cries became more insistent when Hattie did not turn to acknowledge her. "Mama! Mama!"

Hattie hurried out the doors, not daring to look, before she could lose her nerve.

Inside the church, Olive's voice echoed with abandonment.

Chapter Twenty-Four

Hattie and Jeb arrived back at the devastated ranch later that evening. The sun had begun to sink in the west. A tired, bedraggled Mavi stirred something in an iron pot over a campfire. "Where's Brooks?"

"He be in the tent, yellin' at that bandito. Been at it most of the day." Mavi waved in the direction of the army tent where Francisco remained a prisoner. "Mister Brooks sent the deputy back to town. I been tryin' to save what I can from the house. Ain't much left." As Jeb went to unsaddle the horses, she called to him, "Hurry back and eat, Jeb. We got beans and cornbread. You too, Miss ... Missus."

"Maybe later."

Hattie hurried into the tent. Someone had brought out an iron bed frame and placed Francisco on it. He had been handcuffed to the headboard again, and Brooks stood next to him, his face a mottled red with rage. On the bed, Francisco turned to look at her. His bruised and bloodied face showed Brooks had been using his fists to get answers.

"Brooks, Stop!" she shouted as her husband pulled back his fist to send it crashing into Francisco's cheek. "No!"

"Hattie, get out of here."

"No! You stop!"

"Hattie ..."

"No, no, no!" Hattie grabbed Brooks' arm and tugged her strong-willed husband outside the tent. He resisted every inch of the way, but she wouldn't let him loose. "You can't do this. He's going to keep shut up the way you're goin' on. Let me talk to him. He trusts me."

"No."

"He can't hurt me. He's handcuffed to the bed. Let me at least try."

"He hasn't told me anything," Brooks stood in sullen determination. "Why should he tell you?"

"Because I rode with him. I cooked for him and washed for him. He was my … my family. Let me try. Please, Brooks?" Hattie stood on tiptoe so she could reach his cheeks. Touching him gently, she tugged his face close to hers and kissed his stubborn, tight-pressed lips. "Please?"

Brooks shook his head as if washing his hands of the whole thing. "Fine, try. He's not going to tell you anything he wouldn't tell me."

Hattie lifted the tent flap and went back inside. She found a wash bowl on a small table and wet the edge of a towel. Going to sit on the side of the bed, she wiped Francisco's bloody lips, although he flinched. "Go away," he muttered.

"Stay still," Hattie said, wiping off the side of one eye where blood had dried in the night. "I'm not going anywhere."

"So, you married the Golden Star and now you are like him. Rafael would call you a *renegada.*"

"No, I'm not a turncoat," Hattie glared at him, clenching the damp towel in her lap. "I just decided I wanted to live a good life. I wanted to be free like Rafael and you promised I'd be."

How did Brooks say it?

"I want to be like good people who don't take from other people, who don't steal or cheat or kill. I want Olive to grow up loving people, not being filled with hate."

176

"Ha!" Francisco gave a short laugh. "Why do you care so much about a baby you stole from an orphanage? You will not be allowed to keep her."

"I will keep her and love her. Brooks will love her too."

Francisco gave a snicker and shook his head. "You fool yourself, Hattie, if you think this *Golden Star* will let you keep a stolen baby. If he says he loves you or this baby, it is a lie."

"You're wrong," Hattie wiped more blood from Francisco's pulpy, swollen lip. When he winced in pain, she winced too, remembering how more than once he'd put salve on her wounds after Mateo whipped her. "Brooks loves me, I know. I wasn't rightly sure I even knew what love was until I got Olive, and now Brooks. It's a good feeling, Francisco. It fills up your whole heart, an' there's a joy. Not like what we had with Mateo and Rafael. Not like being so filled with hate and going around killing people."

"We did not kill anyone. Did you ever see me lift my rifle to kill?"

"Maybe we didn't shoot the bullets, but we let Mateo and Rafael kill and didn't try to stop them. Kind of makes us the same as they are." Hattie had never told Francisco the story of the pretty teapot with the violet on the lid.

As she got up to rinse the bloody towel, she found herself telling him the whole story in a quiet voice. "That woman didn't do anything bad. The only thing she did was get in Rafael's way because of his hate. She died, Francisco, her an' her whole family."

Francisco jerked at the handcuffs and the iron bed rattled. "Go!"

"Remember how you promised if I went and got Brooks back to Beaumont, I could be free, live a life of my own?" He

177

refused to look or answer, but Hattie knew he heard. "Maybe now it's time for you to be free too. You never liked what they did, Francisco. You taught me my letters and how to ride an' shoot. You never touched me wrong ... not like I didn't want a man to touch me. You weren't like them then, and you aren't like them now."

"Fine words," Francisco sneered but only in a halfhearted way.

"Guess this is like a crossroads," Hattie went on, wringing out the towel and draping it over a wooden chair. "Remember when Mateo always said, we got to a crossroad, we got to choose one road or another? Goin' down a road with him meant somebody got killed or hurt or stolen from. But maybe there's other roads too. Maybe this time we got to decide, do we want to go free, or do we want to follow Rafael? Guess you got a choice."

Francisco kept silent.

"Brooks plans to follow that map tomorrow and fight Rafael. I aim to go with him."

"No, Hattie! You must not!"

"Why?" She walked to the tent flap, knowing Brooks stood just on the other side. "If Brooks is going to die, I will die with him. Maybe then I really will be free of Rafael and Mateo."

As she pushed up the canvas flap, Francisco rattled the iron bed, trying to free himself from his captivity. "Hattie, you must not go with Brooks. The map is to an ambush – when Brooks goes, he will be captured and there will be a showdown in another place."

Hattie had figured as much. She knew Rafael's devious ways. "Then where is the real location? Where does he really plan to attack?"

Francisco shook his head, jerked the handcuffs keeping him tight to the bed. "Brooks and Sheriff Storey are to survive the ambush, but no one else. Rafael has another location for a showdown. Another place where he will fight to the death – Sheriff Storey first, and then, when Brooks is to the point of death, he will be hanged, just like Mateo."

"Where?"

"Why should I tell you? Rafael will kill us too." Francisco stared off at the canvas walls of the tent. "You should let your Brooks kill me now. I am already a dead man; Rafael will never let me live. Or you."

"Maybe this time we can be free? Brooks can ..."

Francisco gave a short, strained laugh. "How will I be free? My freedom will be prison or a rope around my neck. Your Brooks, he knows this. So why should I help him?"

"Maybe if you help us, Brooks will put in a good word for you."

"I have no hopes." Francisco paled and he lay back on the bed, eyes closed. "Either way, I will die."

"Maybe you got no hopes," Hattie screamed at him, clenching her fists, "but I do! I want Olive to be free and live a good life. I want to be free of Rafael and the gang, to be a good wife to Brooks, to maybe have babes of my own. Don't let him destroy me and you, and all of us, like he's destroyed so many others! Mateo was just a ruthless villain – he was *no one* – but we can be good people. We can fight him. Help me, Francisco! Help me."

Tears streamed down her face. "Please, Francisco, help me. Help *us*."

After several long minutes of silence, broken only by Jeb calling to the chickens outside and a far-off howl from a coyote, Francisco turned to face her. "I will die, but you and little Olive must live. Only for you will I give you the right location. I promised you would be free, and Francisco Avila keeps his promises." He sighed. "You will tell your Brooks Shanton I will tell him where he must go."

Hattie hurried from the tent to find Brooks. He stood just past the tent flap, waiting, stern-faced. "He gave me the real location. The map on the rock is an ambush place. Anyone who goes there will be killed except for you and Sheriff Storey. You will be taken to the second place where Rafael plans a showdown."

"I heard him. Are you sure you can trust him?"

"Yes." Knowing Brooks had overheard the conversation, Hattie couldn't bring herself to question him about Olive. *Not just yet.* "Did you hear me tell him you would talk to a judge or somebody, so he doesn't hang? Can you?"

"I can't promise you that it will help," Brooks answered, losing some of his stiff, righteous manner, "but I can promise to try. There aren't many things I can deny you, Hattie."

Hattie smiled as his arms closed her in a safe circle against the warmth of his chest. Under her ear she could hear the steady beating of his heart. "Brooks? Will you promise me one more thing?"

"What's that?" he murmured as he planted kisses on top of her head.

"Let this be the last time you're the Golden Star. When you capture Rafael, let this be the last time you go after someone. After tomorrow, promise – promise you'll take me an' Olive back to Louisiana with you."

He didn't come right out and answer, but Hattie had a feeling she would get her way ... as long as they lived past tomorrow.

Chapter Twenty-Five

"Go back to the ranch, Hattie."

Brooks rode along toward Beaumont with Hattie on a borrowed horse behind him. Although it did no good, he repeated himself every few miles. "Go back, Hattie."

"No."

Sighing, Brooks held the reins and tried not to think about what lay ahead. He'd spent an aggravating night trying to talk Hattie out of accompanying him to Beaumont and the showdown with Rafael. This morning, she'd dressed in her old worn pants, tan shirt, and sombrero, climbed into the saddle, and followed him away from Sam's devastated ranch. Even Francisco, left behind under Jeb's careful eye and fully loaded Winchester, had begged her not to go. Other than tying her up somewhere, Brooks could see no way to leave her behind.

Despite the seriousness of the forbidding morning, he chuckled to himself.

If you wanted a risk-taking wife, Brooks Shanton, you've got one.

"Hattie ..."

"You might as well quit tryin' to get me to go back. I know what they'll do better than you. If you gotta be the Golden Star and go after Rafael, least I can do is help keep you from getting your fool head shot off. Might be I want a husband who stays alive."

Michael had gathered his deputies, as well as many townspeople, in front of the jail. As Brooks rode up, Hattie tagging along behind, he felt a surge of hope at the size of the crowd.

"Brooks, Hattie," Michael greeted them as he mounted his Palomino. "As you can see, we're ready whenever you are. We're ready to help take back our town."

Voices from the crowd rang out. "Lead on, Sheriff Shanton!" "Let's take Beaumont back from the banditos!"

Horses shuffled, snorted, and pawed, eager to join in the fight. The women of the town stood on the board sidewalks, faces taut with worry, fear, or righteous indignation. The calico – red, yellow, green, blue – of their dresses lent a cheerful aura to the somber scene. Somewhere a baby cried, and a door slammed shut as running feet thumped along the boards of the sidewalk.

"Tell us what to do, Brooks," Michael said. "We'll follow your lead."

"The deputies will head toward the ambush point first," Brooks instructed. "You men, be aware that the banditos will try to gun you down as you ride into the ambush. Hattie will ride behind – *well* behind –"

Hattie, I can't believe I'm allowing you to do this.

"Hattie will explain a few things to you about how these men might try to ambush you." To Hattie's credit, Brooks had to admit her knowledge of the gang's movements was invaluable. Last night, they'd sat around a campfire while she gave him every scrap of information that might help.

He let her explain who would be where and who to watch out for, while he glanced over the crowd, looking for the weakest links. From experience, Brooks knew a posse was only as good as its least capable man.

"When you reach the hills, there will be a path between two rocky outcroppings. Avila's men will be perched in those rocks, waiting to ambush anyone who tries to go through. Try to take them alive if possible. If not – use your best judgment."

Nods of understanding appeared throughout the crowd. A few men holstered revolvers. Others checked bullets in gun belts. One of the women began to sob in loud hiccups, and another murmured as she patted her back. Father Kemp stood on the edge of the crowd, his weathered face stern as he muttered prayers under his breath.

"Hattie will lead the townsmen in a different direction, past the ambush point, toward the secondary place where Rafael hopes to accost me." Brooks looked over at Hattie's grim face, chalky with uncertainty. There was no need to warn her about what might happen if the banditos turned on her. Perhaps Hattie knew better than he did the depths of their hatred.

"Do you have your revolver?" he asked her. For just a second, he allowed himself to remember how he'd ask Hattie for a demonstration of her shooting skills last night. While she'd never make a hired gun cringe, she could shoot fast and straight, a skill she attributed to Francisco's teaching.

He prayed she wouldn't have to demonstrate it today.

The townsmen grouped their horses behind Hattie. At a nod from Brooks, they rode down the dirt road, past the weeping women and out of town. Father Kemp raised his hand in a blessing and sadly shook his head. A cloud of brown dust rose behind them, and Brooks could only hope it wouldn't alert Rafael to their plans.

"Let's go, men!" Brooks kicked a booted heel into his horse's flank and edged in front of the deputies. Michael rode close behind him.

The ambush point, a rocky path between two high outcroppings of rock, had been chosen well by the banditos. Anyone trying to ride past would be in perfect target range of their rifles. If those failed to stop any rider, stones could be thrown, or boulders pushed down the rocks to create an obstacle in the path. According to Hattie, there would only be Edmundo and Frank – the two names left on his list – at the ambush, because they were the best shots. The others would lay in wait for anyone who lived to pass the ambush point.

"I'm not rightly sure where Rafael will be," Hattie had admitted, biting a corner of her lip. *"Francisco says he wants to make sure you survive the ambush, so he might be waiting there to catch you. If he is, he'll be behind Edmundo and Frank. You watch for him."*

"They're going to be waiting for us on the path," Brooks stopped the men before they reached sight of the men waiting to ambush them. "Michael and I scouted around yesterday; there's a way to go around and behind the narrow path. Chester, you and Jackson ride toward the ambush. The rest of us will try to catch them off guard." In silent agreement, the two lone men rode down toward the ambush, while Brooks, Michael, and three deputies circled behind the path and crept up on the banditos, perched in their rocky hideouts like vultures.

Gunfire pierced the air. Brooks clenched his teeth and spurred his horse to ride toward the rocks. He managed to arrive just as Edmundo lifted his rifle and attempted a point-blank shot toward old Chester Dutton. "Chester, look out!" Brooks pulled his Colt, ready to end Edmundo's life if necessary to protect his man. He wasn't close enough to get off a shot before Edmundo's rifle retort split the air.

"Chester!"

Thankfully, Chester slipped on a slide of rocks and the bullet ripped out the side of his new leather vest, instead of into his stomach. Chuckling like a mad man, the grizzled old man rolled over like a mountain lion and managed to grab the butt of Edmundo's rifle. Brooks slid across the loose shale, scrambling to help, but it wasn't necessary.

While Brooks had hoped to take the banditos alive, if possible, Edmundo made a bad choice. As Chester grabbed Edmundo's rifle, the bandito clenched it tight, fighting, and stepped backward, toward empty air at the edge of the cliff. His piercing scream as he fell to his death down the rocky outcropping tightened Brooks' heart.

"Toss out your weapon and come out!" Michael shouted from behind another rock. "Brooks! I've got Frank cornered!"

Scrambling over rocks and down a path, Brooks went to his friend's aid. He hunkered down behind the rock next to Michael. "You think he'll surrender?"

Michael shook his head. "Frank! Surrender!"

Frank's revolver shot out an answer. Michael's gun responded, and Frank dropped, blood seeping through the front of his dirty flannel shirt. Michael and Brooks hurried to the man but could see he only had minutes left.

"Rafael?" Brooks stared down at Frank. The bandito, with a last effort, tried to spit into Brooks' face, but all the effort did was spew spittle down his coarse, bearded chin. A gasp, a cough, and the man's brown eyes opened wide in horrible torment as he took his last breath. Despite knowing Frank had a hand in murdering Emily and his boys, Brooks felt only regret. *I thought I'd feel glad when I got vengeance for them.* The last two names were crossed off his list, but he felt only emptiness inside.

The rest of the deputies swarmed up the rocks, checking possible hiding places, guns drawn. "No sign of anyone else," Chester called out as they all heard the unmistakable ricochet of gunfire across the hills.

Hattie!

Brooks, Michael, and the deputies swarmed down the hills, sliding on rocks, sending shale and stones into boot-slipping avalanches before them. Brooks slid and fell, feeling a rock pierce his left hand as he scurried down the hill. Before the others were halfway down, he managed to grab his horse, mount, and spur the animals into a gallop.

Hattie!

When he reached a small copse of trees, his fears flipped to joy as he saw Hattie, well protected behind a big boulder. A man from town stood beside her, a rifle perched on top of the boulder, firing into a field. Hattie sat on the ground, hunched up with her face in her hands.

"We've caught everyone, Sherriff," the man said as Brooks dismounted. "Bert and Johnson rounded up five of them and got them tied nice an' tight over behind those pines. All except that skinny little feller behind that big cypress over there."

"Who is it?"

"Rafael," Hattie whispered through her fingers.

"Rafael Avila!" Brooks shouted. "Give up now. You're surrounded!"

Michael rode up and dismounted and, pulling his gun, he came to stand behind the boulder beside Brooks.

Rapid Spanish split the air as Rafael told them in no uncertain words what they could do with themselves.

"I'm going after him." Brooks said, grabbing at his horse's reins and mounting in one swift motion. "Cover me."

Hattie's *no, no, no* echoed in his ears as he rode toward Rafael's hiding place, not even trying to hide. *This must end. Now. Today. If I don't take him, someone else will shoot him after he kills me. It will end, one way or another.*

To his dismay, Brooks saw he had underestimated Rafael. While riding toward where he thought Rafael had been hiding, he realized, too late, that it was someone else who had been firing at them. To his left, Rafael burst from a wooded area on horseback, weapon cocked.

"Die, die, die!" he screamed, the horse charging at Brooks.

There wasn't a second to think, to prepare. Brooks drew his Colt and, with practiced ease, shot for Rafael's black heart. The bandito clutched his chest, gun still in hand, and a stricken look crossed his face. As the blood drained from his dark, rugged cheeks, Rafael tipped and fell sideways off the horse. His arms flailed, his body thumped to the ground, and the horse ran off, riderless, until one of the deputies grabbed the reins.

Hattie's screams echoed in his ears as Brooks jumped from his horse and went to stand over Rafael's body, Colt in hand. In an instant, he was surrounded by the others – Michael, Chester, several of the townsmen, and Hattie, who clung to his arm and wept against his back.

"He's dead," Brooks said, unnecessarily. Remorse gripped his heart. *Such a waste.*

Michael clapped him on the shoulder, a broad grin splitting his face. He looked around at the other men, their faces showing signs of relief or satisfaction. They'd been given their lives back, Brooks knew, but it gave him no satisfaction.

"Well, men," Michael commented, "you've just seen the famed quick-draw of the Golden Star."

Several of the men congratulated him, patting him on the back and offering hearty and heartfelt thanks.

"I wish he'd given up," Brooks murmured, although only Hattie heard. In a louder voice, remorse tingeing every word, he spoke to everyone. "I wish he'd given up. That he hadn't been so consumed by hatred. There's no joy in seeing such a young life snuffed out."

No joy. Justice had been done for Emily, Sam, the boys ... but at what cost?

It's over, but not done. This will haunt me forever.

Chapter Twenty-Six

"Are you sure you want to do this?" Brooks asked as he stopped the buggy in front of the Beaumont Jail.

Hattie nodded, despite a gnawing ache in her stomach. It would be awfully hard to see Francisco behind bars. Although Brooks had allowed her to go to part of the trial, and she'd even been called one day as a witness, it had been a few weeks since she'd last seen Francisco. Thanks to Brooks, the judge had given him a reduced sentence. Still, he faced years in prison, and Hattie hated it for him. Francisco had always prized being free, treasured being outdoors and sleeping under the stars. To think of him caged in a tiny cell hurt her heart in the worst way.

"It's just gonna be hard," Hattie mumbled, adjusting Olive's pink, ruffly bonnet over her blonde curls. The baby reached up to pat Hattie's cheek, making little *blub, blub* sounds. Hattie righted the tiny lace collar on Olive's pink dress and swiped an edge of her green calico over the baby's already shiny black shoes … anything to put off the second she'd have to get out of the buggy. "You reckon Olive looks good?"

"You don't have to go in," Brooks reminded her, his hands steady on the reins as if one word from her would be all he needed to shout giddyap to the horse.

"I know."

While she still sat in the buggy, Brooks reached out to catch hold of her hand in his. Hattie marveled all over again how strong and fine he was. How he'd brought her and Olive into town last night and told them to buy anything they wanted at the mercantile. While Hattie had never had any trouble *taking* what she wanted, it felt different to have Brooks *buy* her pretty clothes and a bonnet, to watch his smile as he delighted in Hattie's choices, his eager, almost boyish pleasure in having her purchases wrapped in brown paper and tied up in string to carry back to the hotel.

"You're looking right pretty this morning, Mrs. Shanton," he teased, "with that fine new bonnet and dress. I reckon that was the best three hours I ever spent in the mercantile. Well worth the time to have a beautiful wife to squire around town."

"Oh, you," Hattie blushed, aware how the new straw poke bonnet with dark green ruching around her face made her eyes look even greener. *I'm pretty,* she'd thought as the storekeeper's wife brought a mirror so she could try on bonnets and hats. Brooks had stood off to the side, holding Olive, an adoring look on his face.

Even Mrs. Jenson, the shopkeeper's wife, had noticed and teased, "You've captured one handsome man there. He'd buy you the moon if he could."

Hattie hadn't wanted the moon – a big old cold thing in the sky – But a dark green calico with lace on the collar and cuffs made her feel like a woman, a woman cherished and loved. Hattie had never had those feelings before. Somehow it made her feel like her heart might be a bird, ready to leap up and fly away.

Shopping for the bonnet, with Brooks offering to buy her anything she wanted at the mercantile, had been a new experience. Going to visit Francisco before he left for the prison in Huntsville would be another. Harder, but needful. Just like she'd needed new clothes, Francisco needed to have hope.

"I best go on in," Hattie said. "Hold Olive while I get out of the wagon."

"You don't have to do this," Brooks repeated as he held out his hands for the baby. "We can write him a letter once he gets settled."

Hattie shook her head as she jumped out of the wagon. It wasn't quite as graceful a leap as it should have been. Wearing skirts to her ankles would take getting used to but Hattie was determined to be a fine lady one day. "No, I got to talk to him." As if to make Brooks understand, she stood beside the buggy and reached out for Olive. "Francisco was always good to me. When I'd be beat or crying, he'd maybe find me some wild strawberries, or take me fishing. I didn't know then, but I guess I figured out he gave me hope. I got to try to give him some."

Brooks nodded, handed Olive over the side of the buggy. "I'll be waiting."

Hattie carried Olive up the two wooden steps into the Beaumont jail. Taking a deep breath, she opened the door into Michael Storey's office. Michael, sitting with his booted feet on his desk, exclaimed, "Hattie! Don't you look right pretty today?"

Again, Hattie blushed, not used to the compliments. "I came to see Francisco before he leaves. If that's all right."

Michael dropped his feet to the floor with a loud thud. He stood and reached for a set of keys on a peg beside a wooden door with a barred window. "Sure enough. Come right this way. "He unlocked the wooden door and held it open. "The prison wagon should be here in a bit, but you'll have a few minutes to say goodbye."

Goodbye.

Hattie walked into a tiny, airless hall with two cells. Francisco stood from a threadbare cot and walked the two steps to the bars. Already Hattie's heart ached to see him so caged, tears burned her eyes. "I come to talk to you, before you leave."

Francisco nodded but didn't speak. His dark eyes had a haunted look and he already seemed to wither before her eyes. Prison would kill him, unless Hattie could give him something to live for. "Ain't it fine how Brooks got a reduced sentence for you? An' Brooks told me how he talked that judge up and down to keep him from hanging you. The judge was a mean one, but Brooks told how you helped us find Rafael. How you always took care of me."

The baby shifted in Hattie's arms, turning and looking around at this odd place. She stared openly at Francisco, blue eyes wide but unafraid.

Francisco grasped the bars and said with a voice tinged with despair. "Perhaps he need not have bothered. What is a bandito like me to do with himself when I get out of jail? I will always be a bandito, Hattie. I can never change."

"That's not true," she denied. "You were forced into that life just like I was. You never had a chance to break away and be free."

"No Hattie, not like you. You, my little *Chiquita*, had no choice, but I did. I followed Mateo willingly when I left Mexico. I knew that he was not like other men. He did not want to work, but to steal and kill. He wanted to be evil as some men – like your Brooks – wish to be good. I knew, and yet I chose that life."

"It don't – doesn't matter even if you chose that life before. Everybody can change and be somebody different, if they really want to change." Hattie put a hand over his and held tight, trying to make him understand. "I changed, Francisco. An' now I'm a sheriff's wife – me! – little old stupid Hattie Munn. And I'm a mama to Olive. I want her to grow up and live a good life. To know people don't have to wallow in hate or bitter memories. I want her to know if she does something wrong, she can change.

"We didn't have any family but Mateo and the gang – neither of us – but that doesn't mean we have to stay like them. You changed when you helped me and Brooks find Rafael. You did something good, and it saved you from the hangman's rope. You can change all the way and be good – reform, like Brooks says."

"It is true I do not wish to become Rafael or Mateo. I do not wish my life to end at the end of a rope or by a bullet … but I don't know if it's too late."

"It's not!" Hattie pressed his hand tighter as he tried to wrest it from her grasp. Olive reached out a tiny hand and grabbed a cell bar. "Not as long as you got breath in your body, it's never too late."

Michael walked into the cell area, keys jangling from his hand. "Hattie, the prison wagon is here. It's time to say goodbye."

"Please, Michael, just a few more minutes."

"All right." He left them alone again.

"Francisco, please will you try to think about what I said?" Hattie begged, hoping with all her heart he would listen.

"I will have many years to think of what you say, Hattie."

"You promise?" Tears pooled in her eyes and spilled over. Olive, seeing her distress, began to pat her cheek and babbled, "Mum, mum?"

"Promise you will do it for me and for Olive? Promise you will try to change when you get out? That you won't let Mateo and Rafael steal the rest of your life?"

He reached through the bars to grasp her hand tight in his. Although his hand felt cold, his words were warm and certain. "I promise sweet, Hattie. If you will promise me one thing too."

"If I can."

"That you will have a good life, a *feliz* life."

"I aim to."

She couldn't stop the tears flowing as the sheriff came back in and unlocked the cell, taking Francisco and leading him out to the prison wagon. Hattie stood in the narrow hall, hearing Francisco's leg irons clanking on the floor, the creaks and rattles of the prison wagon, a steel door slamming shut. Hattie could not bear to watch. Instead, she held tight to Olive and leaned against the cold, steel bars of the now-empty cell, shoulders heaving as sobs wracked her body.

"There, there." She hadn't heard Brooks come in, but he took her gently by the shoulders and turned her to face him, pressing her face against his chest. "You're getting Olive all damp with those tears."

She tried to make a joke, saying in a ragged voice, "Well, she's already damp in another place. Oh, Brooks, why does life have to be so hard?"

"Shush, shush." He cradled her against his chest, encumbered a little by Olive, who thought this was a fine new game, tugging at the gold badge on his tan vest. "We did the best we could for Francisco, Hattie. He's going to have a chance to reform, and in a few years he can start another life."

"I know, but it's so hard."

He let her cry for a few more minutes and then led her into the Sheriff's office. Outside, they could hear Michael talking to one of his deputies. Someone laughed and the sounds of the bustling town pressed in: a door slamming shut, a horse's whinny and a child's plaintive cry of "Papa!" Leather creaked and a wagon wheel rattled.

"The last thing he said to me," Hattie wiped at her eyes, brushing tears away from her damp lashes, "was to have a good life. A happy life. And I know how to do that."

"How's that?"

"Let's go back to Louisiana for good. You an' me an' Olive an' ..."

"And?"

How would he take the news?

Chapter Twenty-Seven

"There's a babe inside me, Brooks."

"A ..." His eyes opened wide. "You know for certain?"

Hattie reached out to pull Olive's hands away from the golden badge on his chest. "I know, and you're going to take us all back to Louisiana and work on your ranch. Even if it is a peculiar old place, I reckon I can get used to it if you're there, and our babes."

"If you say so, Hattie." He laughed as Olive reached up to tug at his hat. "And I think you'll learn to like Louisiana just fine. I've got a mighty fine ranch, as you know. Right on the path for wayward women to come pounding on my door."

Hattie managed a short laugh. "You say so too, Brooks Shanton, and I don't want no backtalk either."

"Da da," Olive said for the first time, giving Brooks her gap-toothed grin.

They waited inside until the creaking of the wagon wheels and the metal clanks of the prison wagon faded into the distance. Michael came back inside. "Well, he's on his way to Huntsville. It sure is a load off my mind that the Avila gang won't be bothering Beaumont again. It's all thanks to you, Brooks. What are your plans now?"

"We're going back to Louisiana," Hattie spoke firmly, "to the ranch. And we're going to stay there. Brooks promised when Rafael was taken care of, it would be his last fight."

Brooks nodded. "You heard the lady! I guess that from now on, Michael, you're the Golden Star. It sure pains me in one way to part from it," Brooks nudged aside Olive's curious fingers and unpinned the golden badge from his tan vest.

"But, in another way, I want you to wear it now. I'm passing it on to you."

"No, Brooks," Michael backed away, hands held up to push away the honor. "I don't deserve to wear your badge. I can't."

"Yes, you can. You'll grow into it, just like I did."

With Michael's protests still ringing in their ears, Brooks led Hattie outside the jail. They turned back to watch Michael smile widely as he polished the golden star on his chest. Hattie grinned at her husband and let him help her into the buggy.

The sun beamed down its warming rays, the air smelled fresh, and Hattie felt like she might burst from all the happiness inside. The years would go by fast for Francisco and soon he'd be free. With Brooks' help, she would write to him. They would go back to Louisiana, live a good life, and wait for the new babe to come.

Even though Hattie felt her heart might sail off into the sky being so happy, in the back of her mind, a shadow nudged into her thoughts.

I stole Olive from an orphanage. She ain't really our baby. Brooks ain't really her "da da." He ain't wearing a badge, but he's still gonna be true to the golden star he wore.

***

A few days later, waiting for a stage to take them home, they said their goodbyes to Mavi and Jeb, wishing them well on their new ranch. Surprising some, Sam had made a will that left everything to the Jacksons. Most of the ranch was still in ruin, but Mavi and Jeb were eager to begin fixing it up. Many of the neighbors, old friends of Sam, had offered help.

"I'm goin' to miss the likes of you." Mavi clung tight to Hattie as the afternoon stage lumbered to them, "an' that sweet little baby girl. You promise to come visit, you hear me?" she admonished, then with a wink and a grin she joked, "We'll plant us some right fine tomatoes so's you can earn your keep."

"You visit us," Hattie answered back, although she knew Mavi would never leave her beloved Mister Sam's grave long enough to travel to Houma. A few days earlier, Hattie had gone with Mavi to put flowers on the grave. Another day, Mavi, Jeb and Brooks had gone with Hattie to visit her mother's grave. Jeb promised to carve a fine tombstone to put over it. Mavi promised to put flowers there, same as she did for Mister Sam.

Brooks helped Hattie up onto the stage, then handed Olive up as well. Olive had just learned to wave *bye,* and she leaned out the window with a little hand spinning circles in the air.

As they rode the long road back to Louisiana – back home – Brooks let his thoughts travel the path they'd come. He chuckled and Hattie asked, "What are you laughing about?"

"Oh, I was just thinking, I haven't had a drop of whiskey since that night you fell through my door." He leaned over to put an arm across Hattie's shoulders, glad they had the stage to themselves. "I guess that's one way to get a man to stop drinking for good. And maybe another is to find a good woman, like my sweet Hattie, to give me a reason to go on living."

They leaned in to kiss just as Olive pressed her wet bottom against Hattie's skirt. Hattie's heart tugged again with doomed thoughts.

Oh, Olive.

Life was fine until a day later when Brooks got his serious, this-is-for-your-own-good voice. "Hattie, we're going to stop overnight in a town on the way home. We must make a hard decision."

Hattie, back aching, and tired, felt a cloud of doom settle over her shoulders. "What's that?"

"We need to go to the orphanage in Morgan Ridge and return Olive. It wasn't right to steal her."

"No! You might as well rip my heart out and let me die!"

Hattie fought him every mile of the way, ranting, raving, crying her eyes out. It did no good. She hated him that day as much as she'd loved him the night before. Olive, upset by the emotions of her Mama, cried and fussed as the stagecoach drove closer and closer to Morgan's Ridge.

"I'm a lawman, Hattie. Taking a child is breaking the law. I can't in my heart keep her without trying for us to keep her in a legal way. Before we left Beaumont, I promised Michael I'd set things right. We must try."

"What if they take her away?" Hattie sobbed. "I can't bear it. She's my baby, and yours."

The orphanage folks recognized Olive right away and the matron sure enough recognized Hattie.

"You!" She pointed. Hattie's hair had grown long enough to touch her shoulders, and she didn't look so rough, but no doubt the woman still remembered her frantic pounding on the door that night. "And Myrtle!"

The matron just about ripped a screaming Olive from her arms. Brooks tried to explain, while Hattie sobbed, screamed, and tried to say how much she loved Olive. How she wanted a baby so bad she had to steal one. Brooks offered to adopt her legally, but the matron told them to get lost before she called for the sheriff. It was the worst thing that had ever happened in Hattie's life to leave her baby there, crying out, "Mama! Mama!" Worse than any day she'd ever spent with the gang.

They spent a miserable night in a shabby hotel room, Hattie's arms empty, her eyes swollen with tears. Brooks tried to get her to come to bed, but she sat up all night in a hard chair, lips pressed tight, refusing to speak to him. In the morning, Brooks rented a wagon from the livery and announced, "Let's go get our daughter."

Thankfully, the matron had had time to cool down. "Myrtle," she informed them with a glare, "refused to eat or drink and sobbed herself to sleep. We had quite a disturbing night. I had to call in the doctor to dose her with laudanum before any of us could get a wink of sleep."

It was only Brooks' strong hand grabbing hers to keep still that kept Hattie from scratching the matron's eyes out. *Laudanum!*

Another woman was ordered to bring Olive into the room. At the sight of Hattie, the baby yelled out, "Mama! Mama!" and ran straight into her arms. Hattie held tight, kissing every precious inch of her, and even chuckling at that ever-present damp linen diaper. *Just you try to take my baby away again, you old Wart Nose.*

Brooks led the conversation, introducing himself as the Golden Star, and asked what they'd need to do to adopt Olive legally. "My wife is remorseful about all the trouble she's caused, but she wanted a child so much ..." although it was unspoken in polite circles, Brooks let the woman assume Hattie was barren. A joke, really when he thought of the baby she now carried. He refused to look at his wife when he spoke in a sad voice, knowing Hattie might give away their secret.

"Well, now, Sheriff Shanton," the matron gave them a simpering look. "I suppose I understand how someone who isn't blessed can want a child so badly, and it's obvious your wife loves little Myrtle dearly. Let's see what we can do to make her yours."

Not long afterwards, they were on their way back to Houma with Olive Shanton on Hattie's lap.

As they rode away from the orphanage, Hattie couldn't resist sticking out her tongue and yelling back, "Myrtle, indeed, you old Wart Nose! Her name is Olive!"

"Hattie, what am I going to do with you?"

Hattie grinned up at him from under the new straw bonnet, green eyes sparkling with joy, "I reckon you'll think of something, Golden Star. I reckon you'll think of something."

Epilogue

Four Years Later

July 25, 1872

Houma, Louisiana

Brooks Shanton looked at the calendar on the wall as a smile curved his lips. *Life sure has changed in such a few short years.* He didn't often spend time regretting the past, or even looking back. It was better, he knew, to think about each day and be glad, but he couldn't help remembering how just a few years ago he'd sat in this very room, a dusty, cobweb-infested kitchen, with a bottle of whiskey as his only companion, mourning Emily and the boys – right up until Hattie swooped into his life. He chuckled to himself as he stared at his wife, who was busy mixing pie crust. *Today is four years since my life began again.*

"Did you notice the date?" he asked as Hattie turned to give him a smile, those lovely green eyes sparkling as usual. Today she wore a dark green dress, sprinkled with yellow daisies and green ivy vines. Her shiny blonde hair, grown long enough to braid and coil into a bun on her head, hung down her back this morning like a little girl's.

Hattie came over to him and brushed a lock of hair off his forehead. "I noticed the date yesterday," she teased him, curling his hair behind his ears, "and that's why I decided to bake apple pies today. We'll have a celebration."

"Oh, we will, will we?" He pulled her onto his lap and kissed her soundly on the lips. "I think we should. It's truly one of the happiest days of my life."

For just a minute, her face took on a serious look as she whispered, touching her warm forehead to his, "Truly, Brooks? You don't think about – about them?"

"Yes," he said, "I do think about Emily and the boys, but I know I can't do anything to change the past. Somehow, I think maybe Emily had a hand in you coming to my door that day. These last four years with you and the children have been like I've been given life all over again. I love you, Hattie."

She'd just bent over to give him another kiss when a plaintive little voice called from the cabin door, "Papa, Papa!" Olive stood there, her sturdy little body quivering in indignation. "Today it's my turn to carry the milk pail, but Sammy won't let me."

Behind her, a little tow-headed boy glared at his sister. Sammy, named after Brooks' old deputy, held the handle of the milk pail in a white-knuckled hand, the pail almost brushing the tops of his little boots.

Hattie gave Brooks a quick kiss to the tip of his nose and got up. "Now, Sammy, you know today is Olive's turn to help Papa."

While Brooks watched, Hattie managed to unclench the little boy's hands from the milk pail and hand it off to Olive. Then, to staunch the tears quivering from his green eyes, she tugged the collar of his blue shirt and whispered in his ear. "You can be a special helper to Papa today. I think you are big enough to carry a cookie in case Papa gets hungry milking the cow. Can you do that?"

"Yeah," the three-year-old answered, a smile bringing the sunshine back to his chubby baby face. "Me tookie too?"

"Mama?" Olive began, watching Hattie hand Sammy two cookies. "I would like a cookie, too, if Papa and Sammy are eating one."

204

With her cheerful laugh, Hattie handed Olive an oatmeal raisin cookie, too, and shooed them out the cabin door with her yellow, flour dusted apron. "Out, out, all of you! I've got baking to do!"

Brooks grabbed up his son, oatmeal cookie crumbs lining his mouth, and followed Olive, the milk pail clanking down each wooden step as they hurried out of the cabin. He and Sammy shared the cookies as they headed for the barn and their morning chores. The barn smelled of sunshine, baked hay, the not-unpleasant scent of cow hides, and the pungent aroma of a stall that needed to be mucked. Olive abandoned the milk pail and went to do what she considered "her" chore – spreading feed to the chickens.

"Papa? Why you do dat?"

Brooks smiled down at his son, his heart overflowing as always for such a precious gift. "Well now, Sammy, you like to drink milk, don't you?" When the little boy nodded, Brooks scooped a measure of grain and poured it into the feeding trough to keep Ruth still while he milked.

The brown, short-horned cow nudged him with her head, then turned to munch the grain. The little boy's green eyes, so much like Hattie's, stared at everything with a fresh, open eagerness.

George and James, you would have loved your little brother.

Pulling up the three-legged stool and the milk pail, Brooks sat down beside Ruth. "Since you like milk, we have to get Ruth here to give it to us." After a pat to the cow's side, Brooks began the gentle rhythm of pulling and squeezing the milk into the pail. A barn cat came at the first sound of the liquid hitting the tin sides. "Hey, there, Sarah," he smiled at the little gray tabby, glad for her help in keeping mice out of the barn. "I'll pour you a saucer as soon as I'm done."

"We po' sauc'a soon as we done," Sammy repeated in his baby lisp, a promise Sammy kept after the pail foamed with milk. He sat the cracked saucer down, then Brooks handed him a dipper of milk and Sammy tipped it out for the cat. The little boy, short legs scurrying in brown pants, tagged along as Brooks put the milk pail in the spring house to cool.

By the side of the cabin, Olive clucked in imitation of her mama feeding the chickens. "Here, chick, chick," she called, her hands tossing feed every which way. The chickens scurried around, pecking the ground for breakfast.

Midnight snickered from the small corral beside the barn, reminding Brooks of his presence. "You'll get your hay, too," he said. Brooks walked outside, picking up a pitchfork, and scooped up a mound of hay from the haystack to toss into the corral.

Sammy trailed along, as he did most days when Brooks took care of the barn chores. His questions were never ending, but Brooks had never minded the sweet voices of his children, even when Hattie hollered they were about to drive her out of her mind. Brooks cherished every second with this second chance at a family – although he did admit that those two a.m. feedings made a man wonder why babies were so much work. Even when he grumbled to have a night's rest undisturbed, he didn't mean it.

"We've been through a lot the past few years, haven't we, fella?" He patted Midnight's sun-warmed flank and leaned against the top rail of the corral fence. Sammy tried to pull himself up to pat the horse, so Brooks gave him a hand. He'd just sat Sammy on the top rail of the corral when Olive came racing over to join them.

"Papa! Papa!" Olive hollered as she hop-skipped across the yard, scattering the flock of chickens before her. Her pink calico dress fluttered around her legs and, as usual, her feet were bare and muddy. The small yellow braids Hattie carefully tended and tied with pretty ribbons each morning were undone. Olive's yellow curls tumbled around her flushed cheeks, and she brushed them impatiently out of her blue eyes. A tomboy at heart, Olive loved nothing better than climbing trees or riding the pony Brooks had bought her.

"Whoa, slow down," Brooks cautioned as Olive cantered to a stop, out of breath. "What are you in such an all-fired hurry for?"

Like her brother, Olive clambered up on the corral fence so she could pat the horse. "I fed the chickens and went inside, but Mama said I was to come outside and bother you for a while. She said she's worn out from noisy children and wants a little quiet."

"She did, did she?" Brooks smiled in the direction of the cabin – a much larger cabin these days. *Filled with my family. Life sure is different than that day when Hattie and Olive fell through my door.*

"How come you're smiling like that, Papa?" Olive asked.

"Oh, I guess I just felt like smiling," he answered, brushing Olive's stray curls away from her flushed cheeks. "Today is a special day and I know a secret."

"Tell me," Olive begged. Beside her Sammy begged too, "Me, Papa, me tell."

Olive gave her brother a withering look. "No, Sammy, if it's a secret you can't tell. Can you, Papa?" Then realizing she really wanted to know the secret, she changed it to, "Well, you can tell me 'cause I won't tell anybody else."

Helping both children down from the fence, Brooks bent down, so they were all eye to eye. "If I tell you the secret, you can't tell Mama. At least not for a little while yet. Do you promise?"

Olive nodded. When Sammy appeared not to understand, she grabbed his ears and made him nod up and down. Satisfied, they'd promised, she whispered. "We won't tell Mama a word. Not a word."

"Remember when John Pierre brought a letter last week? Well, it was from a friend who told me he's coming to visit us today."

Olive's little lips curved in displeasure. Brooks could almost hear her thoughts. *What kind of a secret is that?* "It's someone very special and I want you both to be on your best behavior when he comes. We can't tell Mama yet though. It must be a surprise."

Brooks knew his daughter well enough to know Olive didn't much like this secret, even before she asked a grumbly question.

"Is this the kind of friend where Mama's gonna brush my hair and make me wear a fancy dress?" Her little eyes opened wide at the horrors that might await, "and shoes? Do I gotta wear shoes?"

"Shoes?" Sammy repeated, although he rarely went anywhere – even to bed – without his small brown cowboy boots. *Just like Papa's,* he always said, and sobbed uncontrollably when Hattie made him take them off to sleep.

"If you don't want to wear shoes or fancy dresses," Brooks reassured her, "this friend won't mind."

"I like this friend," Olive decided. "What's his name?"

"Michael Storey. Remember I told you stories about him? He's a sheriff in Texas."

Olive nodded. "I remember you and Mama talking about him. An' how Sammy's named after your old deputy. Maybe Mama knows your old secret anyway, 'cause she's making apple pies for supper."

Brooks winked. "Oh, I don't think she knows the secret. She just knows I like apple pie and today is a special day. Now, you two rapscallions go play somewhere and don't bother Mama for a while. I've got to mend the fence where the cows broke through in the south pasture. If you see Michael coming, ring the dinner bell so I hear."

"Papa, how come it's a special day?"

"It's the day I met your Mama." Brooks saddled Midnight, watching as the children went to play a game. His heart felt full, and the pain of the date July 25th no longer beat in his mind as the day when he'd found Emily, George, and James dead. Now the date had joyful memories – the day Hattie and Olive fell through his door and into his life. What a glad day that had been.

***

Hattie hummed to herself as she placed two apple pies in the oven of her Franklin stove. She glanced out the window to see Olive and Sammy playing a game they loved – riding a stick horse around the yard. Lily shouldn't wake up for another hour or so from her nap. Earlier, Brooks had said he planned to mend the fence in the south pasture. A glance at the calendar reminded her of the date she'd first met Brooks: July 25th.

Time to sit a spell and remember.

Hattie knew she'd never be as smart as her husband. She'd never had any schooling at all, although Brooks did his best to help her learn to read better and do sums.

With the help of Miz Landry and Miz Watkins at the plantation, Hattie figured she'd learned how to be a right good housekeeper and mama, and by the time Lily was born, she sure had mastered those linen diapers! Babies took a powerful lot of those before they could use the privy like anybody else.

She knew she'd never be as smart as Brooks in book learning, though. Brooks' mind was sharp as anything and he could think things through in a way Hattie knew she'd never try. Hattie didn't rightly understand all what he meant, but she knew she learned more each day as Brooks' wife. When he explained things, they seemed to make a lot more sense.

They'd talked a lot about how his first wife and sons died. "*You coming to me on the same date,*" Brooks had explained once, "*makes it like a circle. From the tragedy of that day six years ago, to the happiness we have now.*" Hattie liked that idea, and something else Brooks always said: "*Good can come from evil, Hattie, just sometimes it's a mighty hard road to get there.*"

Hattie sighed, sat in her rocking chair, and closed her eyes, enjoying the slight breeze coming in through the window. Maybe it was like Brooks said, and there was a God somewhere looking out for them all. Maybe He'd been there all along when her Mama sold her to Mateo Avila and set her life on a hard, dangerous road. After all, if not for that road, she may never have met Brooks.

A smile curved Hattie's lips as she thought of her strong, handsome husband. It had taken her a while to get used to the idea that he wasn't going to abandon her or mistreat her. That he loved her – dumb little old Hattie Munn, whose Ma didn't even want her.

Hattie especially loved the nights they lay in one another's arms, their heads sharing one pillow as they whispered in the dark. It had taken years of such nights for her to feel safe and loved. On more than one night she'd shared her life with the gang as Brooks wept with her.

"I'm so sorry," he'd say, his face wet with tears that mingled with her own. "Sorry I couldn't save you a long time ago." Having Brooks understand made up for all those awful years she'd been alone and afraid with just Francisco to look out for her.

As she rocked, looking around her clean, well-swept cabin, Hattie smiled at all the nice things Brooks had bought her. Every so often, she looked around and knew how blessed she was to have the life she had now. Oh, she loved her "pretties," as Miz Landry called them, the fine walnut China hutch with pretty China – even a teapot with a violet on the lid – the calico curtains fluttering at the windows, chairs with soft cushions, and kerosene lamps with glass globes of fine white porcelain painted with yellow roses. But Hattie knew she would not mind losing those things. Like Mavi had taught her long ago, they weren't as important as her precious Brooks, Olive, Sammy, and Lily.

"Mama! Mama!" Olive hollered from outside. "I see a rider coming from the south."

Hattie sighed. Although she dearly loved all three of her children, she had to admit that some days being a *mama* got tiresome. Although, as she often told Brooks, it was a sight better being a mama than riding with a gang.

Hattie walked out onto the porch and stared off to the south. It was impossible to tell who the rider might be from this distance, but in the past few years she had learned not to jump at every visit from a stranger. Those years with the Avila gang had marked her for a long time after, but with Brooks' love and their children, she had finally put the past behind her.

"Mama!" Olive jumped from the tree where she'd been keeping watch. "Papa said if anyone came, I was to ring the dinner bell so he could come. In case anyone came."

As the rider grew closer, she could see the broad white Stetson and knew it must be Michael Storey coming for a visit. It wasn't often Michael rode the distance from Beaumont to Houma, but he was always welcome when he did. Now that he had two younger deputies and a bride of his own, he tried to make the journey once a year to visit his old friends.

"Well, then," she told Olive, "ring the dinner bell while I put the coffee pot on."

Hattie bustled inside the cabin, wiping floury hands down the yellow apron. Outside she heard the *clang, clang, clang* as Olive jerked the iron dinner bell side to side. Smiling to herself, she went to pull open the oven door to check the pies. Sheriff Storey surely did love his apple pie – just like Brooks. And just maybe, he would have news about Francisco.

***

Michael rode up in time to meet Brooks as he came from the corral, alerted by the dinner bell's clang. "Michael! You made it! Your letter was a little mysterious. Why are you so far from home?"

"Well now, that's a long story. I hope you can let me bunk here for a day or so."

"You know you're always welcome." Brooks looked down at the children, staring in amazement at the tall, white hatted man on the golden palomino. "You remember Olive and Sammy? Olive, do you remember Sheriff Storey? He visited last year."

"Well, now, they were no bigger than grasshoppers last year." Michael tipped his hat to Olive who giggled. Sammy, not quite certain about this near-stranger, grabbed Brooks' pant leg and hid his face.

"Hello, Sheriff Storey," Olive had never met a stranger, and her grown-up way of talking surprised many. "Guess what? I'm almost five years old now! My birthday is August first and Papa took me to town all by myself and I got to pick out a present at the mercantile ..."

The words were run together in Olive's usual impetuous way, but Michael seemed to enjoy the prattle. "Is that a fact? Why, I can remember last year, when you were only four."

"I was a baby then," Olive's nose crinkled, and she sneered at how young that was. "Sammy's only three, almost four, now and Lily's not even a whole year old yet."

"That's right, I haven't seen the newest addition to the family!"

"Olive," Brooks knew his daughter well enough to know she'd never stop talking unless someone shushed her. "That's enough for now. You can visit Sheriff Storey later. Go tell Mama we've got company for dinner."

"She already knows that Papa, she saw him, same as I did before I rung the dinner bell. Then she went inside to make coffee."

A stern, "Olive," buttoned her lips.

The little girl stopped, hurt, but knew better than to argue. Brooks gave her a smile and a chuck under the chin to soften the blow. "Take Sammy with you."

"Well look at that big boy," Sheriff Storey said as Brooks drew the little boy away from his tight hold on his pant leg. "He's grown since I've seen him."

"He's three," Olive informed him again, eager to get across this necessary information. "He won't be four for months and months. C'mon Sammy, let's go tell Mama what Papa said."

Reluctantly, Sammy grabbed his sister's hand with a fearful look back at Michael. He tugged his brown pants up with the other hand and followed Olive, almost stepping on her heels.

"That little Olive sure speaks her mind, doesn't she? Sounds a lot like her Mama. What'd you ever do to have such sweet kids, Brooks?"

Brooks laughed, once the kids were out of distance of hearing, he joked, "Well we stole one from an orphanage. The rest are homegrown."

Michael laughed at the private joke, knowing his friend's secrets as well as his own.

They had decided Olive would never need to know the truth about her birth.

"I don't want her to think somebody didn't want her from the start," Hattie had said as they rode away from the orphanage on that long ago day, *"We loved her from the beginning and that's all she needs to know."*

"What are you doing out this way? No trouble, I hope?"

"No trouble at all. I had a chance to be out this way and since it wasn't that far from you all, I decided to pay a visit. See that new little one Hattie wrote to me about. And I wanted to bring that *present* I wrote you about."

Brooks grinned, anticipating Hattie's pleasure in the present.

They shared the local news from Beaumont and Houma as they walked toward the cabin and the delicious aromas of pot roast and apple pie.

"Michael!" Hattie threw her arms around him and hugged him hard. "I think I knew we'd be havin' company today. I put on a special company meal this morning and baked pies. I'm so glad to see you. Come, sit, tell us about everyone in Beaumont. Olive, set the table. Sammy, you help her."

As the children hurried to put plates, cups, and silverware at each place at the big wooden table, Hattie couldn't stop talking. She dished up pot roast, potatoes, and a bowl of creamed peas.

"Do you see much of Mavi and Jeb?" Hattie bustled around the kitchen, pulling a pan of warm biscuits from the oven with a dish towel.

Michael sat at the place Brooks motioned him and accepted a hot cup of coffee in a fancy glass cup. "Doing fine, doing fine." He took a sip and leaned his bulk back in the chair, spurs clanking on the wooden floor. "Jeb comes for a visit every week or so when he's in town. You wouldn't believe the improvements they've made on the ranch. Jeb decided to raise cattle, and they've got a fine herd now. They fixed up the big house just dandy. You wouldn't recognize the place."

"I'm glad." Hattie set a dish of butter on the table and grabbed a China pitcher of milk.

At his chair, Brooks delighted in watching Hattie's happiness in having fine things like China. Hattie had never asked for fancy furbelows or fine China – but he knew how it delighted her.

"Mavi sends her regards. Says you all should bring the children for a visit someday."

"Mavi wrote me they took in some children. How's that working out?" Pulling out Sammy's chair, Hattie lifted him into his seat and tied a towel around his neck. She quickly started serving dishes around the table, helping the children fill their plates. Cutting up Sammy's meat and buttering a biscuit for Olive, she kept her bright, inquisitive eyes focused on Michael's face like he might vanish, like she was hungrier for news of their friends than food.

"They did indeed," Michael helped himself to the pot roast and passed it to Brooks. "Mavi said since they couldn't have any children themselves, they'd help others. Last time I went out there were three boys and two girls from an orphanage in the south. You wouldn't believe how those young ones just can't do enough for Jeb and Mavi."

Olive and Sammy were quiet during the meal. Sammy was always shy around strangers, but Olive had never met a stranger yet. When it was just family, Brooks and Hattie let her chatter away. When company came, though, the children were expected to mind their manners. Brooks could tell Olive was having a hard time keeping her little pink lips silent.

Thankfully, Michael must have noticed too. "So, Olive," he said, and the little girl perked up, those blue eyes sparkling, "what did you buy for your birthday?"

"Papa bought me a doll for my very own. I can show you after we eat."

"Well, that's right nice."

Since no one stopped her, Olive prattled on. "Mama said I could name her anything I wanted, so I named her Hattie 'cause it's the prettiest name I know." She grinned at her mother, butter dripping from her chin.

Hattie leaned over to wipe her daughter's face. "I told her there's prettier names," she said in embarrassed delight, "but she's set on it. "

"It *is* the prettiest name there is," Brooks smiled across the wooden table at his wife. Hattie flushed and looked down at her plate.

The meal went on with quiet conversation and ended with warm apple pie, just as Lily set up a fuss from the other room. "Olive, go joggle the cradle a minute until I can feed her. Take Sammy with you. I'll come in a minute."

The children scrambled out of the chairs and went to do as they were told. Both loved nothing better than helping with their baby sister. "You got some mighty fine young ones there." Michael forked up another bite of pie, "and a mighty fine baker in Hattie. I swear, Hattie, if I eat another bite my Angie's going to have to sew my pants bigger!"

Hattie, unmindful of Lily's escalating whimpers for a meal, or Michael's compliment, moved her chair closer to his and asked in a quiet, eager voice. "Have you heard anything of Francisco lately?"

"That's right, it's about time his sentence is over," Brooks said as he took another bite of apple pie. He winked at Michael. "Have you heard anything about his plans? Where will he go? The warden sent me a letter not long ago that Francisco was a model prisoner and he had great hopes of him leading a better life once he gets out."

"Well, now," Michael got a smile on his face, "that's another reason I thought I'd pay you all a little visit." He stood and went to the cabin door. "I sure hope, Hattie, you've got enough of this fine meal to feed another mouth."

With that cryptic remark, he stood on the porch and emitted a loud, piercing whistle. Hattie looked at Brooks, at

Michael, rose from her chair and ran outside. From the bedroom, Olive and Sammy ran into the kitchen, curiosity in their eyes. Sammy looked on the verge of tears and grabbed Brooks' leg to hide his face.

"What's wrong? Mama? Papa? Why did the sheriff whistle so loud?"

Across the back pasture a rider on a black stallion drew closer. Hattie pressed a hand to her mouth as tears pooled in her eyes. A silent word formed on her lips: "*Francisco.*"

Francisco rode up to the porch, dismounted in a hurry, and ran to grab Hattie in his arms. Off to the side, Michael and Brooks watched the joyful reunion. Brooks' heart soared at seeing Hattie so happy. It had been difficult to keep Michael's secret, but well worth it to see Hattie's shining face.

The man who stood on the porch hugging Hattie had changed in the years since they'd seen him in Beaumont Jail. His dark hair had been neatly cut and although his cragged face still bore scars from his years with the gang, a genuine smile creased the hardened cheeks in newfound happiness. Francisco wore clean dark pants and a brown shirt. Instead of the sombrero he'd worn much of his life, a black Stetson topped his head. Without the sombrero, Francisco looked more respectable, somehow.

The children stood beside their Papa, staring in curiosity at this stranger. Sammy whimpered and snuffled a runny nose against Brooks' leg. Inside, baby Lily announced to the world that she better get her dinner, and soon!

"Francisco, Francisco," Hattie half cried, half muttered the name, hugging him so tightly the man looked on the verge of having his breath squeezed out. "I missed you so much!"

"Mama," Olive interrupted, tugging on Hattie's apron, "Lily's awful hungry."

"Oh my!" Hattie let Francisco go, wiped her tears with the yellow apron and apologized. "I have got to feed that baby. Brooks, you give Francisco some dinner. Now, don't you go anywhere."

Francisco shook his head and crossed his heart. "Michael has offered me a job with him in Beaumont. We are going to stay a few days and have a nice long visit before we leave." He laughed, a sound like bells ringing out. "I am to be a deputy! How is that for a change, my sweet Hattie?"

Hattie, tears filling her eyes, couldn't speak as she went to feed Lily.

Brooks shook Francisco's hand. "We meet under better circumstances this time. I'm glad things worked out for you."

"As am I." Francisco's leathered hand shook Brooks' hard. "And grateful to have such a friend."

He turned to look down at Olive's inquisitive blue eyes. "And who is this? Do not tell me this is Olive? Baby Olive."

"I'm not a baby," Olive declared. "I'm almost five years old."

All the men laughed. "So you are, and do you know something, Miss Olive?"

Olive shook her head.

"You were my inspiration these past few years."

"What's he mean, Papa?" Olive tugged at Brooks' hand, uncertainty wrinkling her brows. "What's 'spiration?"

Brooks and Michael laughed. Francisco squatted down to speak to her eye to eye.

"It means I changed my life because of you, *Chiquita*. You are the reason I wanted to breathe fresh air, to be a free man and live a changed life. Because my sweet Hattie told me the next generation must grow in love and not hate. When life grew hard, little Olive, I thought of you and how you must have a better life than your mama and I did when we were young. We were taught to hate, but you and your brother are taught only love."

"Did you know my mama when she was little?"

"*Si*. We grew up as banditos together."

Olive took great offense at this and drew up her little body, fists clenched. "My mama was *not* a bandito! Not ever. My mama is good."

Brooks could see this conversation had clearly upset Olive. Especially when she turned to him, lips quivering, "Papa? Mama was not a bandito, was she?"

Having heard his stories many a night, about his years as a sheriff fighting banditos, Olive knew banditos only as very naughty people who got justice from her Papa. Although he kept his stories mild for little ears, Olive and Sammy both knew banditos were bad. He knew his daughter well enough to know this was not how she pictured her beloved mama.

"Well ..." Brooks wished the conversation had not come up, but he knew he'd have to be honest. "Your mama *was* a bandito." At Olive's gasp, he thought of a way to ease out of the uncomfortable subject until she grew old enough to know some of the truth. "Your mama was the very worst kind of bandito," he said as Hattie came back out on the porch with Lily in her arms. "She stole my heart and never gave it back. "

"Papa!" Olive squealed, annoyed at this, but not upset about *this* kind of bandito. Running to grab her mother's skirts, she tattled, "Mama, Papa said you were a bandito and stole his heart."

Hattie smiled down at Olive. "I reckon he's right. But that makes him a bandito, 'cause he stole my heart too. Now, you two run off and play so Francisco can have his dinner and we can talk."

"Mama and Papa were banditos!" Olive hollered. "C'mon, Sammy." She grabbed her brother's hand. "Let's go play." As the children jumped off the porch, Brooks reached for Hattie's hand and squeezed tight. Scattering chickens across the dusty yard, Olive kept up her silly shouting, "Mama and Papa were banditos!" Tagging along, Sammy managed a lisped, "'Ditoes! 'Ditoes!"

"We best not take her into town anytime soon," Hattie cautioned. "People might get the wrong idea about us. They think I'm a mite strange anyway."

Brooks often told Hattie how good could come from evil, but sometimes it was a mighty hard road getting there. As he thought of everything evil had done – the deaths of his wife and sons, Sam, and all the waste and heartache the Avila gang had caused, it seemed like there was no hope at all in the world. That the road would grind them all to dust on the trail.

But as he looked at Hattie, smiling as she introduced Lily to Francisco, he knew they had survived all the tragedy and regrets of the past. Four years ago, Brooks didn't think he could endure another minute, another breath. Today, he hoped he'd have years and years to count his blessings.

July 25, the best day on the calendar.

THE END

Also by Zachary McCrae

Thank you for reading "**Justice on Horseback**"!

If you liked this book, you can also check out **my full Amazon Book Catalogue at:**
https://go.zacharymccrae.com/bc-authorpage

Thank you!

Printed in Great Britain
by Amazon

32826694R00126